THE BOIS DE VINCENNES

NIGOGHOS SARAFIAN

THE BOIS DE VINCENNES

NIGOGHOS SARAFIAN

Translated from Western Armenian by
CHRISTOPHER ATAMIAN

With an Introduction by
MARC NICHANIAN

THE ARMENIAN RESEARCH CENTER, UNIVERSITY OF MICHIGAN–DEARBORN 2011

English translation of *The Bois de Vincennes,* copyright © 2007, 2011, by Christopher Atamian

Distributed by Wayne State University Press, Detroit, MI 48201

Manufactured in the United States of America.

15 14 13 12 11   5 4 3 2 1

Cataloging in Publication Data
Sarafean, Nikoghos.
[Vensēni antaṙě. English]
The bois de Vincennes / Nigoghos Sarafian ; translated by Christopher Atamian;
introduction by Marc Nichanian.
77 p. :ill.; 23 cm.
ISBN: 1-934548-02-2
ISBN13: 978-1-934548-02-8
1. Armenian literature—translations into English.
I. Atamian, Christopher.
II. Nichanian, Marc, 1946-.
PK8548.S25V46 2011
891'.99235—dc22

Paper used in this publication meets the minimum requirements of the
American Standard for Information Sciences—Permanence of Paper in
Printed Materials, ANSI Z39.48-1984
Edited by: Wendy Warren Keebler
Cover art by: Linda Ganjian
Cover and book design by: Savitski Design
Publishing Consultant: Alice Nigoghosian

A special acknowledgment and thanks to CNRS Editions, France, for providing
the illustration of Nigoghos Sarafian.

This book is dedicated to the memory of my father, Georges Atamian, writer and patriot. — *Christopher Atamian*

ACKNOWLEDGMENTS

Thanks to everyone who made the publication of this book possible and supported me in one way or another during the long process of translation: Esther Allen, Jean-Marie Atamian, Nigol Bezjian, Denis Donikian, Georges Festa, Linda Ganjian, Matthew Hensrud, Nanor Kenderian, Marc Nichanian, Neery Melkonian, Silvina Der-Megeuerditchian, Sofia Milonas, Alice Nigoghosian, Ara Oshagan, Ara Sanjian, Sophia Seidner, Aris Sevag, Hrag Vartanian, Svetlana Yasinskaya, Heidi Weisel, and Nathaniel Wice.

This book would not have been possible without the efforts of the Armenian Research Center of the University of Michigan-Dearborn and the generous support of the Ajemian Foundation. Thanks as well to the readers, friends and others who provided invaluable suggestions and comments as the final manuscript was taking shape. Finally, although every effort has been made to insure accuracy, errors that remain are mine alone.

"The task of the translator consists in finding that intended effect upon the language into which he is translating which produces in it the echo of the original. . . . The traditional concepts in any discussion of translations are fidelity and license—the freedom of faithful reproduction and, in its service, fidelity to the word. These ideas seem to be no longer serviceable to a theory that looks for other things in a translation than reproduction of a meaning."—*Walter Benjamin*, "The Task of the Translator" (introduction to a Baudelaire translation, 1923; text translated by Harry Zohn, 1968)

"Our homeland has escaped us. She slid beneath our feet, throwing us out to sea. But that's the best way to learn how to swim." — *Nigoghos Sarafian*

CONTENTS

FOREWORD
Ara Sanjian

NIGOGHOS SARAFIAN'S *The Bois de Vincennes* is widely acclaimed as one of the most important texts of twentieth-century Armenian Diaspora (or diasporic) literature. Since its first printing in Aleppo, Syria, in 1947, the Armenian original of this highly praised work of prose has been reprinted a number of times. Interestingly, all Armenian editions have either been serialized in literary periodicals or have appeared in collected works of the author. Previously, only the French translation of *The Bois de Vincennes* was published under separate cover. This English translation is the second such publication, underscoring its uniqueness and importance.

When Christopher Atamian's English translation was first submitted to the Armenian Research Center (ARC) at the University of Michigan-Dearborn, all experts contacted by us for their opinions welcomed the idea of having *The Bois de Vincennes* available in English. We were not surprised when we were also warned almost immediately that this was an intricate work and that translating it into English would be a real challenge. Sarafian's style is complex, and his language is ornate, with frequent allusions to symbols from the rich Armenian cultural heritage, going back a few thousand years. The ARC invested a lot of effort in verifying the accuracy of the translation. What is especially important for us at this stage is to bring this celebrated work of a pivotal figure in twentieth-century Armenian literature to the attention of the international English-reading public and also to the growing number of ethnic Armenians in the United States and other English-speaking countries across the globe, who are no longer able to read fluently in the native language of their ancestors.

The ARC is also fully cognizant that Armenian literary critics have read and analyzed this work through many lenses. In order to acquaint general readers with the world of Sarafian before they immerse themselves directly in the enchanted world of *The Bois de Vincennes*, the ARC agreed to the translator's choice of including an English-language adaptation of Marc Nichanian's introduction to the French translation of this work.[1] We thank Varoujan Arzoumanian of Éditions Parenthèses in Marseilles, France, for granting us permission to publish the adapted English translation of this introduction in our edition. Readers who are interested in exploring further the depths of Sarafian's literary world are encouraged to look into other critical analyses of *The Bois de Vincennes* and of Sarafian's literary output in general. Unfortunately, very little is available in English to date about Sarafian as secondary literature; readers fluent in Armenian and French are luckier in this regard.

Sarafian wrote in Western Armenian, the branch of the Armenian language that is spoken by those Armenians whose ancestors lived in the Ottoman Empire until the genocide of 1915–1916. The pronunciation of some consonants in Western Armenian differs from that of their counterparts used in Eastern Armenia (of which the territory of the contemporary Republic of Armenia is part) and from the way these consonants were pronounced back in the fifth century, when the Armenian alphabet was created. Although it is common in English-language academic publications to transliterate Armenian names according to the principles of classical-cum-Eastern Armenian pronunciation, the ARC decided to diverge from this tradition on this occasion and adopt a transliteration based on Western Armenian pronunciation.

I wish to thank those scholars who provided the ARC with various forms of advice and assistance in the process of publication of this translation. Finally, heartfelt thanks go to the Ajemian Foundation, which subsidized the publication of this work in memory of Robert Ajemian.

Ara Sanjian
Director, Armenian Research Center
University of Michigan-Dearborn

---

1   Marc Nichanian, "Sarafian la Conquête de l'Exil," in *Le Bois de Vincennes*, trans. Anahide Drézian (Marseille: Parenthèses, 1993), pp. 7–16.

TRANSLATOR'S INTRODUCTION
Christopher Atamian

AS I PREPARED to enter the Air France boarding area at Charles de Gaulle
Airport late in August 2007, the writer Denis Donikian piled some books—a
few of them his own—into my arms. A slim green paperback volume caught my
attention, the French translation of Nigoghos Sarafian's *The Bois de Vincennes*.[1]
Seeing that I had picked up this book from among the dozen or so that he
had given me, Denis murmured in his inimitable French way, "They say it's a
classic. I find it completely maddening and unreadable, but there you go." With
such an introduction to the work, how could I not be fascinated? I read it from
cover to cover, ninety pages in all, on the flight home to New York and was
mesmerized by its complex imagery and remarkable personification of a park on
the outskirts of Paris. I had never read anything quite like it in modern literature,
Armenian or otherwise. Everything about *The Bois de Vincennes* seemed slightly
odd to me: its poetic prose style—perhaps partly derived from the work of the
Constantinopolitan-Armenian mystic writer Indra[2] and also its contents, a dicey
mixture of descriptions of nature and Armenian history mixed in with impressions

---

1   Nicolas Sarafian, *Le Bois de Vincennes*, translated from Western Armenian by Anahid Drézian (Mar-
     seille: Editions Parenthèses, 1993).

2   Born Tiran Chrakian in Constantinople, Indra (1875–1921) was one of the renowned Armenian writers
     of the early twentieth century, in the wake of the Realist movement. His masterpiece, *Nerashkharh*
     ("The Inner World"), published in 1906, is a fascinating mix of philosophical musings and mystical
     reflections; the reader cannot but be struck at times by the similarities in style and content to *The Bois
     de Vincennes*. Indra gave up writing soon thereafter to become a preacher. He survived the depreda-
     tions of 1915 only to perish six years later on the road from Konya to Diyarbakir, deported by the
     Kemalists in 1921.

of wartime bombings and quasi-philosophical musings on everything from history to women to the act of writing itself. Anahid Drézian had done a remarkable job of rendering these issues, as well as Sarafian's very particular style, into contemporary French.

Once I found myself firmly ensconced again within the comfort of my Upper West Side home, I paid a visit to Columbia's Butler Library to find the Armenian original. I was not disappointed. I fell in love with the author, perhaps like the Lebanese-Armenian writers of the previous generation, who, as Marc Nichanian avers, discovered in Sarafian a writer who could render the world in a modern, sophisticated way, a writer who could so accurately describe the diasporan psychology of dislocation, all of this in Western Armenian. I fell in love with his imagery as well, with the expressionistic elements in his awesomely unrelenting extended personification, with his way of alluding even to the Armenian genocide or Catastrophe in ways hitherto unseen:

> Some trees are troubadours, while others sing canticles. There are priests who swing censers and shake fans, while pagan cantors and plane trees await together the arrival of a prince. There are also poets and heroes of the revolution. And sometimes when a storm explodes ferociously out of nowhere, the trees are an entire people massacred and sent into exile, their women and children screaming in the wind.

Most of all, I identified with Sarafian's engagement and battle with the notion of doubt and the absence of certitude, which I have always found to be one of the most challenging aspects of human existence:

> I always doubted the lessons they taught us in school. I doubted whether the train would ever leave the station. I doubted whether I had locked the door when I left my house. I questioned whether the metro headed to Porte Maillot might take me instead in the opposite direction to Porte Champerret. Or that the tunnel walls weren't about to close in and trap the subway car deep within the earth's bowels. I didn't have an ounce of confidence in architects.

Translating from Western Armenian[3] into English presents a daunting challenge. With the exception of those in the Middle East, most Western Armenians do not learn this language in school, and when they do, they don't study it in what linguists term a "natural" way. Even when they learn it concurrently with the host country's official language, English or French, the latter remain their mother tongues and Western Armenian the language into which they translate these other tongues. It is a problem that Sarafian himself was quite aware of. Translating Sarafian, then, is an exercise in both love and frustration—it means constantly referring back to dictionaries and thesauruses and sending e-mails to colleagues and friends in far-off places such as Beirut and Aleppo in order to verify a certain word or expression. It makes the ultimate result, of course, all the more satisfying. It is my hope that English-language readers of this book—Armenians and non-Armenians alike—will discover the beauty of another culture and world, perhaps another way of thinking. It is also my hope that some of these people will be inspired to learn this rich, wonderful language—Western Armenian—a language on the verge of dying out. And finally, it is my hope that, despite all predictions to the contrary and despite the grievous harm done to it as result of the Turkish will to annihilation, which almost destroyed a language along with its people and culture, Western Armenian may someday soon experience a Renaissance.

---

3   Armenians today learn and speak two main versions of the same language—similar but different enough to be sometimes mutually unintelligible. Armenians in the Republic of Armenia, Karabagh, and Djavakhk (in southeastern Georgia) speak Eastern Armenian, based on the dialect of the Ararat Plain in the nineteenth century, while the majority of Armenians in the post-1915 diaspora, who originate from the Ottoman Empire, speak Western Armenian, originally standardized in Constantinople, again in the nineteenth century. Speakers of Western Armenia predominate in the Republic of Turkey, Lebanon, Syria, France, and other countries where large Armenian communities formed after 1915.

INTRODUCTION: Sarafian and the Conquest of Exile
Marc Nichanian
(Translated from the French *by Christopher Atamian.*)[4]

THE BOIS DE VINCENNES is many things simultaneously: a meditation by an exiled poet on his unique destiny and on the equally unique destiny of his people; a reflection on the West, and an attempt to integrate the notion of exile into language itself. First and foremost, however, it is one of the most beautiful twentieth-century texts written in the Armenian language.

Published in 1947 by Nigoghos Sarafian, an author who had already been living in France for twenty-five years, this poetic meditation requires a few introductory remarks, as the historical context of its genesis is almost wholly unknown to the Western reader. It is true that a few examples of Armenian literature are available today in their English translations, but these books usually arose from an entirely different context from the one at hand. This is one of the rare occasions when the English-reading public is being presented with a literary work that belongs entirely to the Armenian diaspora, a unique entity in more ways than one and which Armenians themselves would be hard-pressed to characterize in accurate detail. Sarafian and a few of his Parisian contemporaries tried the best they could to make sense of

---

4   *Translator's note:* This introduction by Marc Nichanian originally appeared in French and preceded Anahid Drézian's French translation of *The Bois de Vincennes* (*Le Bois de Vincennes*, Nicolas Sarafian, Marseilles: Éditions Parenthèses, 1993). It was written for a French reader and remains the most in-formative and expertly written explication of this particular work. Hence it made the most sense to present it, with as few alterations as possible, to the English language reader as well.

the singular situation that they found themselves in; hence the status of the literature they produced was also unique.

Thus, while Sarafian's entire *oeuvre* is written in Armenian, his work does not come to us from Armenia itself; nor does it speak to us of a lost country, located far away in space or time, whose borders we might be able to trace on a map or perhaps in someone's memory. It is without a doubt the work of an exile but one without a country or a past. In particular, it offers no exoticism to latch on to or to refer back to.

I will now attempt to explain this somewhat complex situation. By mixing historical events, biography, the history of language, and some thoughts about the difficulty of translation, I will try to unravel this meditation on exile, which was particular to Sarafian and, through him, his entire generation.

Born in Varna, Bulgaria, in 1902, Nigoghos Sarafian spent his childhood in the European part of the Ottoman Empire, on the shores of the Black Sea, in the town of Rodosto, now known as Tekirdağ, Turkey. Having survived the stormy days of the early twentieth century that were so deadly for his people, he ended up in Paris in 1923, as did many of his compatriots, and he remained there until his death in 1972. He lived his entire adult life in Paris, which is where he wrote books in his native tongue, Western Armenian. In *The Bois de Vincennes*, however, Sarafian writes that he didn't unequivocally feel Armenian to be his own language and that he had only come back to it after "having become a stranger to myself in a foreign school." In Paris, he published his books, was a discreet witness to his century, and experienced its many convulsions.

Sarafian's youth was similar to that of his Armenian contemporaries, victims one and all of the same destructive will of the Ottoman authorities, both before and after the coming to power of the Young Turks in 1908.[5] Thrown with his brother onto the roads of Bessarabia and the Crimea from 1915 to 1917, while

---

5   Among recent works that study in depth the annihilation of Armenians in the Ottoman Empire are Vahakn N. Dadrian, *The History of the Armenian Genocide* (New York: Berghahn Books, 1995); Donald Bloxham, *The Great Game of Genocide* (Oxford: Oxford University Press, 2005); Taner Akçam, *A Shameful Act* (New York: Metropolitan Books, 2006); Ronald Grigor Suny, Fatma Müge Göçek, and Norman M. Naimark, eds., *A Question of Genocide* (Oxford: Oxford University Press, 2011); Raymond Kevorkian, *The Armenian Genocide* (London: I. B. Tauris, 2011).

his people disappeared into the Catastrophe[6] that destroyed the Armenians of the Ottoman Empire, Sarafian returned alone from the killing fields of the Russian Revolution to wind up in the Ottoman capital of Constantinople, now under postwar Allied occupation. (Some of the scenes in *The Bois de Vincennes* recall, some thirty years later, the horror of a young boy faced with cartfuls of dead soldiers.) The Armenian institutions of Constantinople had been relatively spared, out of the Young Turks' desire to keep up appearances until the very end. Constantinople is where Sarafian developed his love of literature in one of the prep schools where the remaining master teachers who had managed in one way or another to survive the raids of 1915 were teaching once again, having returned one by one to the capital city after four years of unabated terror and underground existence. The most important of these masters was the novelist and critic Hagop Oshagan, a member of the great generation of writers who came to maturity before the war.[7] Oshagan instilled in Sarafian a passion for language and for the rigors of poetry, qualities that would stay with him permanently. Sarafian would furthermore maintain with Oshagan, who died in 1948, the difficult relationship of a rebellious son.

The three years between 1919 and 1922 were relatively calm and saw a literary renaissance of sorts among the Armenian survivors huddled together in Constantinople. It's in this city that the taste and desire for literature were born in Sarafian, as well as in the few dozen or so young refugees studying there under the tutelage of their masters, all of whom would later find refuge in Paris. This period of relative tranquility would also come to an end with the advance of the Kemalist troops in 1922, which precipitated the flight of these remaining

---

6   As I have argued elsewhere, the proper word for the Armenian genocide in Armenian, one that expresses the complete annihilation of a people, is *Aghet* or "Catastrophe," which is the exact equivalent, semantically and otherwise, of the Hebrew *Shoah*; see my *La Perversion Historiographique: Une Réflexion Arménienne* (Paris: Lignes, 2006), recently translated into English by Gil Anidjar as *The Historiographic Perversion* (New York: Columbia University Press, 2009).

7   Immediately preceding World War I, in 1914 Constantinople, Oshagan had published, along with Daniel Varoujan and Kostan Zarian, the literary review *Mehyan*, which has remained a legend in its own right until today. To learn more about *Mehyan* and its importance in the literary history of Western Armenians, see chapter 1 of Marc Nichanian's *Entre l'art et le témoignage: Littératures arméniennes au XXᵉ siècle, Vol. II: Le Deuil de la Philologie* (Geneva: MétisPresse, 2007), English translation forthcoming from Fordham University Press under the title *The Mourning of Philology*.

intellectuals and put an end to the history of Armenian Constantinople as people had known it until then. This moment can be considered the birth of the diaspora.

Sarafian was only twenty-one years old when he arrived in Paris, a city he would never leave. He took on a variety of odd jobs in order to survive, before becoming a typographer at the newspaper *France Soir*. At the same time, he passionately followed the new literary movements that were taking France by storm, including the birth and ensuing turmoil of Surrealism, the history of ideas that was developing (Existentialism and its attendant philosophical movements in particular), and the violent ideological battles of that epoch. Sarafian's concept of and engagement with the entire notion of "doubt," which forms a large part of his thinking about himself and finds echoes in certain passages of *The Bois de Vincennes,* derive from these early years when he had to make sense of the world and acquire a certainty about it as well, all certainties being good and hence in the end equal, for a young man who needed to believe in something in order to believe in himself. One shouldn't think of Sarafian's "doubt" as a natural given, a sort of tempered skepticism, nor for that matter is it the Faustian doubt that proclaims, "And I've read every book there is to read," even if one passage in the book refers explicitly to Faust. Instead, we should understand it as a product of a laborious struggle, the result and the playing out of a tragic confrontation. Writing[8] itself also

---

8   For Sarafian, writing was a Sisyphian task—he says as much when he writes of his "rock" or "boul-der." Sarafian was constantly starting texts anew, rewriting the same poems and sets, the same themes, even the same individual sentences. The final state of his manuscripts is a testament to this fact—he rewrote *The Bois de Vincennes,* for example, numerous times. The essay by Krikor Beledian that introduces his anthology to Sarafian's work, published in Paris in 1988, shows his will to throw himself repeatedly back into the fray. This is particularly true with respect to *The Bois de Vincennes,* which represented an apotheosis for Sarafian and thus an ending as well. Sarafian felt this all the more strongly from the moment that his readers—and Krikor Beledian as well—starting in 1969 onward drew up an inventory of his work and emphasized the singular importance of this particular text, which is itself a self-assessment of sorts: a review of a life devoted to poetry, of an exiled life, and, I would add, the unfinished passing in review of methodical doubt. A life can end. Exile can end. Doubt, however, when it's mixed in with the process of writing and poetic creation, can only remain unfinished, because it is its own negation, ad infinitum. Sarafian is perfectly conscious of this, as evidenced by the fact that he also writes in *The Bois de Vincennes* that he doubts even this conquest, the most difficult of all and one that becomes confused with his work—that is to say, the conquest of doubt itself. Doubt is a terrible drama.

played an important role in this doubt. Still, the human need for certainty would never have undergone this questioning without the self-examination imposed by exile, by the chosen and assumed identity of the stranger as a stranger. Sarafian was not the only writer to do battle with his "identity" as a foreigner, or what could better be called the destruction of identity. He belonged to a generation of young Armenian writers from Constantinople who, like him, had all emigrated to Paris at the beginning of the 1920s. There, in 1931, they formed a literary review called *Menk* ("We"), which expressed, if not a collective will, then at least the desire to represent a new reality, and to embark together on an adventure that previous generations had not experienced. Born of the Catastrophe, forever confronted by the Other, they felt obliged to make sense of the disaster that their fathers had experienced and to integrate within themselves, by way of intellectual effort and by working on their own language, this Otherness that they could not escape.

This category of the stranger or the alien is the dialectical locus that they helped to create but were never completely able to master.[9] One should not interpret this to mean simply a reality that was alien to them. On the contrary, this state of existence was entirely familiar. One also shouldn't construe the term to mean "another identity" that they would have taken with them, an identity that a foreign country or homeland might have conferred on them. If they were in fact strangers in a strange land and alien to the West, this country was by no means alien to them. It is for this very reason that they felt alien to themselves before being so to others. This constitutes, one must admit, a rather paradoxical situation: a state of complete nudity of sorts, a way of being "thrown" mercilessly into the world (the term is Sarafian's), a situation that Sarafian was among the few to expose so completely. They were unable to assume or to bring with them "another identity" because, first and foremost, they carried within them an absence of identity, a hollow shell that ate away at the very possibility of creating any identity. Sarafian says as much in a remarkable sentence in the first issue of *Menk*, when describing his entire generation: "Close, too close to European civilization, it discovered the

---

9   As in *The Bois de Vincennes*, where the category of the "stranger" is seen as feminine, that is, the sexually perverted and fascinating prostitute who is the source of all evil.

emptiness within itself." Having discovered this empty space of nonidentity, which was passed on to them as a cruel and unexpected inheritance, many of these writers tried desperately, incessantly, to escape this fate.

Sarafian and his colleagues had a twofold task ahead of them: to try to comprehend the disaster that they had experienced but also to delve into, integrate, and, they hoped, conquer this impossible nonidentity. Confronted with the destruction of their collective existence, the writers of this generation had to carry forth this double task within language—their own language, that is to say, in the only collective space that had been allotted them.

For all of the reasons I've given, Sarafian's exile was not simply a matter of being physically removed from a homeland. The hazards of biography made it such that Sarafian, even more so perhaps than any other writer of his generation, wasn't born just outside a homeland but also outside that first homeland that is one's mother tongue. Writing was to transform this happenstance little by little, until it became the very essence of his existence as both a human being and a poet. Poetry can only be born of exile. The opposite is also true: poetry can only be about one's homeland. In a letter written in 1910, Daniel Varoujan, the most iconic Western Armenian poet of the early twentieth century, implicitly questioned his most recent work: "Patriotic poems have taken us far from our homeland."[10] Varoujan's goal was to "conquer" the homeland. Less than two decades later, Sarafian's goal was to try to conquer exile itself. In spite of the fact that the writers used different terminology and lived under different historical circumstances, the two projects shared much in common. One's homeland is always in a sense missing, a memory of something it never truly was. Language is precisely this memory one has of one's homeland, and of the absence of that homeland.

Hence exile—the diaspora—like doubt itself, is not a given or fact. Like doubt, it must be conquered, and the instrument of this conquest must be language. It exists in an unstable state or middle ground, a sort of "mediterranean" in the etymological sense of the word, caught between

---

10 Daniel Varoujan (1884–1915) wrote these words on the road that brought him back from Belgium to his native land after many years spent in the West. Six years later, Varoujan would be deported and killed in central Anatolia by the Young Turks. The homeland was murderous.

the metaphorical lands represented by certainty. (In a particularly strange sentence in *The Bois de Vincennes,* Sarafian writes: "caught between the decline of religion and the rise of science.")

Sarafian and his colleagues who founded the *Menk* group, because they were writers, found it necessary to incorporate the paternal disaster and the meeting with the Other into their own language. But perhaps they became writers, craftsmen of language, precisely and only because they lived, more than others, overwhelmed by the urgency of this confrontation. All of the important authors that made up the *Menk* group—Vorpuni, Shahnur, Sarafian, and Nartuni—whose names I am citing here rather than others—felt this same sense of urgency and confronted in their own work, each in his own way, the fatal wound which for them formed the very basis of this group. They needed to conquer anew for themselves and on their own terms the space of language, the clandestine space of exile.

Sarafian's first book of poetry, published in Paris in 1928, *The Conquest of a Space,* inaugurated a modern poetics. This sometimes futurist work inaugurated a modern poetics which only resonate with Armenians, as well as with Sarafian's readers and literary heirs at the end of the nineteen sixties. The forty years separating the book's publication and its literary reception made for a painful reality. Sarafian's solitude, which he imposed on himself, was not only of his own making. His contemporaries were simply not ready to question their accepted ideas or beliefs.

After he published a book of minor importance, *Fourteen* (1933), the modern poetics that Sarafian initiated found its culmination in 1939 in the great work of poetry *Flux and Reflux.* The latter, a trip toward the Mediterranean, toward a fluctuating space of desire, of childhood memories woven in with images of the present, and a luminosity of language as great as Paul Valéry's, possesses a spark and a lightness rare in Armenian literature.

Between 1927 and 1934, Sarafian tried his hand at a new genre, the novel(la), which he eventually abandoned. In 1934, he published a short text, *The Princess,* his only work in the genre to be published in book form. Isolated during World War II, Sarafian went back to writing more traditional poetry, sometimes taking up classical themes, as in his 1946 *The Citadel.* This was the last book he would publish for more than twenty-five years. The veil of silence that existed because of the cultural conditions in the diaspora had taken its toll on Sarafian. These conditions fall under at least three disparate categories that must be mentioned, since they are directly linked to the fate of the Armenian language in the diaspora.

After World War II, Beirut had taken over from Aleppo[11] as the Armenian diaspora's cultural nexus. The Lebanese capital exercised hegemonic control over what was included or excluded from its many literary reviews. As the new capital of the Armenian-speaking world after the dispersion, Beirut was not, however, ready to assimilate and reappropriate the experience of the first generation of writers, the Parisian generation. Beirut was also not ready to admit the paternal disaster of 1915 or to confront the Other within its midst. A second reason for the silence imposed on Sarafian was that, with a few exceptions, his entire entourage had disappeared. There was nothing left of the literary groups, of the passions and intellectual upheavals of the interwar period. The sociological process at work behind the gradual loss of the Armenian language in the diaspora, which eventually leads to the destruction of Armenian cultural existence in the West, are well known. Great poetry requires cultural links, and these were starting to be sorely missing. Finally, and here is another important factor that should not be forgotten: (Soviet) Armenia for the most part ignored the great authors of the diaspora. Few of their books, or even their names, have crossed its boundaries. How, then, could they have penetrated into the Armenians' consciousness?

One has to wait until 1971 for Sarafian's next work to appear. *Mediterranean* was published in Beirut under the impetus of a group of Sarafian's admirers; it was his first book, in fact, not to be published in Paris. What I have previously stated about Beirut also has its flip side. Were it not for Beirut and its active Armenophone community, which transmitted its great literary figures and culture to the next literary generation, and, more important, had there not developed there one last generation of Armenian-Lebanese writers[12] who published their own literary review, *Ahégan* (1966–1970), it is more than

---

11   It was in Aleppo that *Le Bois de Vincennes* was first published in 1947, in the literary review *Nayiri*, edited by Antranig Dzarougian.

12   These include Harutiun Kurkjian, who published an anthology of Sarafian's work in 1982, and Krikor Beledian, who has commented at length on Sarafian's work. Both have since left Lebanon.

likely that Sarafian's work would have disappeared entirely or remained at best a distant literary memory. The young Beirut authors discovered in Sarafian an ambitious poet and thinker, open to the world and to its ideas, a man whose writings perfectly encapsulated the diaspora's many contradictions. They saw in it an attempt to set out and conquer exile. They recognized in Sarafian a noteworthy and talented predecessor, the one person who had successfully taken on the West in the Armenian language, and a writer who had also taken Western Armenian off the beaten track, to a place of brilliant incandescence. *Mediterranean* reprises many of the themes of *Flux and Reflux*—in particular, a passion for the sea, for in-between spaces, for the limit between the solid and the fluid, for the limits of certainty. In *Mediterranean*, the last book Sarafian would ever publish, the author also re-creates the sublime language that characterized his 1939 masterpiece.

Even though Sarafian's literary output slowed down after 1946, he nevertheless published numerous articles and literary fragments in the various Armenian newspapers in France and the Middle East, in particular the Parisian daily *Haratch* ("Forward"). His writings in these pages are those of an intellectual observing his epoch and of a poet awaiting inspiration. Sarafian also published some brilliant essays, of which *The Bois de Vincennes* is but a first example, situated as it is somewhere halfway between poetry and the fragmented writing of literary commentaries. In these writings, Sarafian attempts to recapture his moment of literary glory of 1946, when he achieved a poetic apotheosis of sorts by taking stock of his life and his work and of his age, as well as that of his people's trials and tribulations and finally of his position as an exiled poet. The totality of these writings, which also include a few articles belonging to the genre of the poetic essay, was anthologized in Paris in 1988.[13]

Sarafian is difficult to translate, for a very particular reason, which is a direct result of the uniqueness of the Armenian diaspora, as well as because of the particular status of literature and of the writing of some of his contemporaries.

---

13 One should also mention the 1982 edition of *Poetic Oeuvres* (which doesn't contain Sarafian's essays and articles), as well as a reprinting that saw the light of day in Soviet Armenia during the Gorbachev era in 1988, under the guidance of Alexander Topjian. Topjian reprinted the original text of *The Bois de Vincennes*, which had previously appeared in the second and the joint third and fourth issues of the literary review *Gam* ("Or"), edited by myself in 1982 and 1986, respectively.

The greatest difficulty in translation usually lies in moving from one cultural sphere to another; this is also, paradoxically, the raison d'être of translation itself. Translation lets the reader "see" an author's world through a unique prism: that of a different language, in this case English. Translation is a way of acquiring a fresh outlook on another world. Hence it always depends on the means available to it in the language that a text is being translated *into*. The translator's task is to find these means, at whatever cost, even when they are not readily available. This necessity, this wonderfully grand aspect of translation, is rarely recognized. But the difficulty in making an English translation of Sarafian is twice as great. The reason for this is quite simple: for fifty years—his entire adult life, in fact—Sarafian lived in Paris. One might rightfully ask, what "other world" should translation open one's gaze onto in this case?

It's easy to understand why translation is a difficult art, even within the simplest context, the one where the stranger or "Other" comes from a completely different world: every translation presupposes a natural state of existence of the originating language, a natural difference that the language being translated into (the receiving language) perceives as an obstacle to be overcome, like some unsolvable riddle. In order to translate this natural quality into the translator's language, one must use artificial means. A translation of Sarafian's writing, however, can posit no such natural state of being, since Sarafian's Armenian was already the result of a huge effort of "translation" on the author's part. Call it what you will: a contradictory endeavor, the conquest of exile, the discovery and assimilation of the stranger/Other, the opening of language onto a nonidentity. All of the themes that I introduced in the first part of this introduction can best be understood in light of the act of translation itself. Sarafian took on the difficult task of translating the stranger (or Other) into the self, on the stranger's own terms and territory. Yet that which is already a "translation" can only with difficulty be retranslated. Walter Benjamin noted as much in 1923, in his introduction to Charles Baudelaire.

The difficulty in translating and presenting Sarafian, then, lies beyond empirical facts. The world we must encounter when we read Sarafian is that of exile, that is to say, of a land that remains to be conquered. Armenian diasporan writers do not for the most part possess the luxury of being exotic. The best among them don't aspire to exoticism anyway, nor do they regret its absence. Yet they have always lived within a transparent bubble, writing alongside their Western compatriots while remaining invisible to them. I hope that this translation of *The Bois de Vincennes* will help to burst this bubble and help to show that literature can also be cultivated, expanded, and re-created even within the context of permanent exile.

Or on the contrary, literature might serve as the very locus of this exile.

THE BOIS DE VINCENNES
NIGOGHOS SARAFIAN

Translated from Western Armenian by
CHRISTOPHER ATAMIAN

1

THE BOIS DE VINCENNES extends from the Marne to the Don and even farther down, also covering a large part of the Black Sea. Sometimes it reaches the sky. It goes beyond my nostalgia and my memories. It glides over a utopian and unknown homeland. And on Sunday mornings and summer holidays, amid the consecration of the clarity of the aurora borealis and the sap-colored quivering of its transparent trees, I am transported into the most extreme ecstasy. A ship sailing out of darkness. The grass overflows, extends pure and fresh, and speaks to me. The silent treetops balance themselves, capturing and diffusing light. Shadows lengthen. The air and the earth and the plants are like honey. And through the fleeting shredded clouds and the sad, vain flow of years gone by, I discover the meaning of my childhood excitement when, drunk from the sea, I felt that vague emotion called hope.

But the Bois de Vincennes torments me as well. A tribunal: "Tell the whole truth and nothing but the truth." My heart beats from anger and confusion. And then a rustling of the branches like a terror-filled murmur. A light flashes like an electric current atop the trees. An explosion and then lightning. The shock between negative and positive forces, between child and man, between thinker and worker, between exiled and assimilated, between the beautiful that leads to the ugly and ugliness that moves me as well. The Bois de Vincennes leads me to the most violent contradiction. It becomes a crime-filled battleground. At times, I walk at the bottom of a red sea, in the silence and the lights that attach themselves to my limbs. A sunken world. And the carmine ghost rising from its blood, transformed along with the same monstrous creatures. The sun shines red, the shadows red. At this time, the smell of the trees, dizzying but tragic, slowly becomes oppressive. The birds flee the silent darkness with djinn-like squawks. I can still hear the scraping

of the guard's broom one cloudy day, when he let me gather the gold of the
dead leaves when I was without work. And one hears riding on the wind
the plaintive cry of the sweeper of illusions' wounded pride. The desolation
of fall, beautiful in its decline. Occasionally, a cart goes by full of chopped,
scarred wood, and then it slowly moves on like the one that used to pass by
the train station in Rostov on days when a battle had raged, full of naked, wet
corpses, their eyes wide open. And the trees swaying in the wind and the lush
grass that waves back and forth recall the ship of faith that used to sail up the
long river of hope always to find itself at the foot of some virgin waterfall.
Truth only makes you want to know deeper truth. Every revolution leads
to another. Which is the genuine one? Sometimes I sit down, exhausted.
In front of me lie the underground bunkers, protection against nighttime
bombings, memories of the days when men lived like moles. In front of me,
the abandoned military stations of the victorious troops. Misery. And in the
vacuum, the city's low rumble.

2

THE BOIS DE VINCENNES is enticing. The trees are witches at times,
magicians wearing cruel wooden masks. Demons who whistle in the cold
winter nights, gypsies who foretell the future. A spirit emerges from within a
leaf, and the woods become chaotic under the sun. The entire length of the
forest vibrates with metallic sounds that echo off one another. A landslide
rumbles, and then a magnetic current passes by. The ground trembles like
a Negro in a trance. One of the spirits throws down a gold coin. A horse
chestnut rolls onto a path, bounces back up, and then explodes, letting loose
from its resplendent green skein a shiny fruit that looks up at the world
askew like some crazed, wild colt. The dead leaves lift themselves and flee
like the undulation of a long wedding train. An invisible spirit suffers at
the bottom of a waxen riverbed as the sun's rays embed themselves like so
many witches' needles. And a frightened bird screeches over and over again,
while another one moans, and yet another sings its lamentations to the skies.
One hears the moans of a pregnant woman. And when everything quiets

down and silence descends on these sylvan surroundings, from one end of the woods to the other, a celestial music rises in the air. A child is born. The soft oil of goodness pours from its branches. The trees become wise men bearing gifts, lambs of Christ. The Bois de Vincennes is beguiling.

Buried under a winter cloak of snow, the trees are angels who beat their white wings in the sky. The angels whisper of a lost heaven, and at night they become ivory shrouds, somnambulists sleepwalking through the moonlight. Snow covers them like powdered sugar. And when enough accumulates near the frozen ponds under the setting light of nightfall, the powder shines like a birthday cake and glistens like the New Year's Eves of my lost childhood. The trees are monsters drowning in the autumn rain. In this place, life is a fable. There are trees who tell tales and children who live them. At times the trees form entire armies that do battle mercilessly, sword against sword, horse manes waving in the wind, helmets waving as well amid thousands of wind-beaten banners. Some trees are troubadours, while others sing canticles. There are priests who swing censers and shake fans, while pagan cantors and plane trees await together the arrival of a prince. There are also poets and heroes of the revolution. And sometimes when a storm explodes ferociously out of nowhere, the trees are an entire people massacred and sent into exile, their women and children screaming in the wind. Some trees look like executioners and thieves, while others limp and are hunched over. Some are wealthy, others poor. In the springtime, as in summer, veiled courtesans dance in the wind. One of the willows shakes her large, proud stomach, and her hips vibrate like cords under the sun's rays which reflect out of the water and stream through her long, undone hair. There are trees that know only heartache, while others straddle the sky between their legs. And then there are triumphal arches.

3

THE BOIS DE VINCENNES is magical. Space is abolished. On the shores of the Marne, Varna. Time is suspended, faced with the naked bodies that lie there motionless. And when one of them shakes itself off and starts to move to the rhythm of a modern dance, it turns into a savage tripping to the music like a possessed demon. You begin to understand our century. Space has been abolished. The man who watches the swimmers and the boats glide by also sees in front of him a long-forgotten picture of a foreigner in a small town, in a foreign school learning a foreign language, the language of his new spiritual homeland. Each word that he learned as a child grew inside him with such charm that it made everything he was to experience more beautiful. The child has reached the end of his dream now, and thirty years later, he's become a man who returns in search of his roots amid the days where this dream was born. He stares at the swimmers and the boats, at the buzzing cafés and the Sunday crowd, and at the musicians as well. He also looks at the boy, and an amazing psychological unfolding takes place. One transmits his light to the other, like two people from different worlds telegraphing messages back and forth. And the one's dream, melded to the other's knowledge, for a fleeting instant illuminates the bitter years gone by. One—innocent—waits to be corrupted, while the other—corrupt—wants nothing more than to be innocent again. And all of the words that before were only dreams have become real. The villages and the hills in the old picture have proper names now: Nogent, Joinville, Maltourné, Maisons-Alfort, Saint-Maur, and Charenton. The bridge that the child admired also has a name, the Mulhouse Bridge. And the immobile and colorful people in the picture suddenly begin to move. The woman under a parasol looking up at the sky. The man who won't stop staring at his fish hook. The one reaching for the fish flapping at the end of the line and the one swimming toward a balloon. All of these people and others whom he shouldn't care about anymore touch him deeply because they are a link to the past. While the musicians continue to play, he hears everything, including the silence of the picture itself. He finds happiness even in the lost loves of the musician's song. And always far away, the tricolor waves in the air, just like the one in school when he was a child. And always, floating in the air, his anxiety.

4

AT THE RACETRACK in the Bois de Vincennes, when you watch from afar, the horses look as if they're running along a tree crest. And as the sun shines brightly down on this crest, it transforms itself into a glowing powder under the horses' sparkling hooves. And little by little, countless branches stretch out like hands toward rolls of paper money. A silver rain shines down in a delicate, sensual shiver. Hope and enthusiasm, bad luck and bitterness as well. Life is a race to success, and the jockey within each one of us must learn to deal with all sorts of games: with corruption, with good and bad luck, with hustlers and women who strut their stuff on the grass and graze about impudently, ever beautiful and foolish.

A long time ago, I used to walk by here on my way to work. Early in the morning, upon leaving the woods, my eyes would fill with tears like those of a condemned man as I walked in front of the houses and the passersby. At night, on my way back home, I would take a shortcut through this dark world and keep my eyes fixed on the lights inside the houses.

Behind all beauty lies ugliness. Behind every social climber lies a sorcerer, an expert in the matter. And by the time we are old enough to see and understand corruption, we've already been corrupted ourselves. But beauty also lies behind all ugliness. We love women although we know that they're nothing but blind desire. Art is also a drug: the enchantment of being able to explain away evil and the drunkenness of an inner ravishing, the act of courage of the man who bathes in a monster's blood and in so doing becomes untouchable. A test: the willpower to defeat the wicked through one's own innocence.

On that day, as traffic extended from the city to the woods and from the woods back to the city, a roaming crowd overran every pathway and expanded in every direction. Not one corner remained silent. The woods weren't a convent anymore or a place to talk, a reception room or a world of marvels. Cars whizzed by like arrows. They pierced the luminous world of dreams and ripped through the shadows. The gravel paths groaned underfoot, and the tender grass lay crushed under the weight of so many thousands of bodies and feet. Men and women rolled around on the grass intertwined, kissing, laughing, and yelling. Children ran through the bushes, mimicking their elders, and yelled as they raced their toy boats.

At times, I liked this human tide. Were these memories of some ancient pilgrimage or the drunkenness of youth? Or maybe love for the pastoral life? Or joy for humanity freed from work and slavery? Or perhaps nostalgia for pagan times when orgies of sexual liberation brought about true bliss? Women are beautiful when they lie down under the trees with their legs exposed. They're beautiful when they sit on the grass and lean back on their long alabaster arms. Their breasts perk up, their stomachs flatten out, and in this extended position, as on their nuptial beds, they resemble virgins waiting for their men to undress slowly. I liked crowds, once upon a time. In the streets of the big city, I gave myself up to the electric energy that these endless bodies produced. I became drunk from the ocean-like sound of their endless steps. But little by little, as the years passed, this same crowd threw me into a deep solitude, because I recognized the difference between them and myself. And I was alone in my difference. One night, on a pavement slippery from the rain, in the lights that sparkled at the bottom of a dark mirror, I suddenly felt like a stranger dangling over the abyss. But I also experienced an even more daunting evil. The earth was alone, floating in space. Human beings were also alone and adrift. And at the same time, there were no more individuals left. I thought to myself that man must have been this way since the dawn of time: walking, talking, eating, copulating, laughing, crying, sacrificing himself. Always in pursuit of an illusion, waiting for a future that never arrived. The sidewalk boiled under my feet, the decay of thousands of years of existence. And I walked along a pavement wet from the blood of a thousand crushed worms, alone and adrift, wondering what was still to come: a holy chrism or an infernal ointment? And the lights from the luxury boutiques—red, white, green, and yellow—illuminated the millions of raindrops and covered pedestrians with one large funereal mask, as if they were all dead. The lights reflected off the wet pavement and awoke several generations of dead medusas and slithering, salacious snakes. I had seen civilization, my adolescent dream . . . I had seen it and lost myself in it . . .

Today I prefer the solitary woods. And I'm sad when I find them littered with pieces of paper, old food, potholes, and broken branches left by the passing multitudes. But within me, the crowd is always reduced to its most essential nature. Should we deduce from this that we remember precisely the things that we try to forget and that we feel we need the most? The crowd is responsible for my deception and my injury and also for my desire to rise. And from afar sometimes, it's beautiful as well.

The Bois de Vincennes is infinite.

5

ONE DAY, a purebred galloping wildly in the woods caught my attention. His mistress, a beautiful young woman, kept screaming, "Mercury! Mercury!" Was there love in her voice or anger? Was I witnessing some enticing drama, or was she simply goading him? Then, as she passed by me, she threw a flaming lasso around my neck; I pulled back and in turn drew her nearer to me. The victor in love or in poetry is actually the loser, and any loser is really the victor. And the entire proceedings had a noble aura about them. But behind this giving of oneself lay just another egotistical, deceitful conquest.

The horse made a large circle as he approached me and then galloped away. From time to time, I saw the woman balance herself on her mount and yell behind hanging branches that continued to sway after she had disappeared again. I heard her cry and the sound of the hooves hitting the ground and the sound of my own heart's hooves that refused to reduce her love to common, vulgar words. I watched in romantic awe, a leftover from my teenage years. I used to love femmes fatales: beautiful and cruel women who neither led you on nor discouraged you, disdainful women whose desires burned like a scorching rock. I used to enjoy suffering. Is it possible to exist without this particular torment? I was in love with love itself, with the goodness that it brings, with the heart's outpouring, with its spiritual communion. And this contradiction led me straight to chaos. Light and shadow did battle. Dust glistened on leaves, and rays of light streamed out from the tree trunks, bounced off the hot metallic summer sky, and came gushing forth in an infinite, burning splendor. The air sparkled. The horse trotted by a pond one last time, and the light reflecting from it made his eyes glisten for an instant. The sight of water made him open his mouth. He reared up and shook himself. His chest shone in the light, strong like a blazing bronze statue. The young woman kept her grip firm around his neck. I caught a glimpse of a handsome face, and rather than fear, I sensed a desire to dominate etched on it. I saw her sculpted neck, her chest, and her strong, bare arms. Her scarlet nails and lips shone in the sun. A diamond sparkled on one of her fingers like a crystallized version of her soul. I loved her, and I loved this steed. I had spent my childhood with horses. One day, one of them pulled the reins out of my youthful hands and sped off, dragging me off in the cart behind him. I remember the graveyard wall where he stopped and the gutter where the cart finally came to rest on its side outside the city limits, facing the sea. And this sylvan apparition troubled me and excited me and shook me to my core. But the horse and the young woman disappeared. And the echo of the horse's hooves gradually diminished and then disappeared completely. I remained, empty-handed.

Sometimes I think that I can still feel the warmth of their blood and the beating of their hearts. Sometimes I even think that I see them in the woods when the wind hits the trees and the raindrops sparkle on each individual leaf like diamonds or the horse's eyes. But now I am mainly a man of thought and judgment. And what I actually discover in the woods is the light emanating from my own eyes as it gets to the bottom of things. A powerful, blinding light. I hear the sounds of his hooves, but I can't see the horse anymore. I think back to my youthful enthusiasm and dreams, although I realize that they are all illusions. The passing years are a terrible waste, an insane deterioration, and these old dreams offer us the only consolation for life's vanities.

I move forward, weighed down by my visions, and live in fear of my own impotence. We expect happiness from both love and poetry. And in order to be happy, we must have faith and await something that never arrives. We must be duped. This is the only way that I can justify to myself the young man who was, now that I have no more justifications. I've become what I was meant to be, while before I was merely developing. A desire to start life over again? Not really. Each path ends in the same place—six feet under. Yet I long for innocence lost, for craziness and goodness, and for burning desires in order to be free to live, to create, to love, and to smile. I love life even though I don't know how to grab hold of it. I long for calm, and this desire becomes a storm within me. I revisit the boy that I once was, and I don't envy him. . . . I hate what I wrote yesterday, in spite of the joy and exaltation that it gave me at the time.

6

ONCE UPON A TIME, for many years before and after work, I would seek out the intimacy of the trees. There were my benches and roads that led off the beaten path, moving right to left and north to south, cutting through this forested world. Sometimes I would sit and watch the cars pass by. Swallows. At other times, I would penetrate deep into the woods, far from them, with the same joy as an explorer. A search. A long wait for unknown messengers. A love of solitude, in which one can also read a certain arrogance and timidity. Homesickness. And the woods restored my strength after a hard day's work. I remember wondrous evenings and nights filled with mystery, books waiting to be born . . .

But everything is different today. None of my dreams lasts. My pleasure is a fruit plucked with sorrow. And I am sad even as I enjoy myself. Always that dreaded fear of fooling myself. I lie down on the grass. In the end, one gets tired of everything except the need for tenderness and beauty that becomes an obsession as one approaches death without having found either. I enter the woods in order to forget myself. There's so much self-hatred in my loneliness. I possess every vice. It's useless trying to find succor in other people's misery. Sometimes I take my face into my hands, like Cain. I wait and I wait for a tear to roll down my cheek and remind me of some past greatness. And as the grass mystically transforms itself into a field of light, as the sun creates an abstract path in the sky and the trees become immaterial, I am tortured by a dark sunlike specter.

Doubt.

My thoughts contain the seeds of their own destruction. When I look at an ant today, I don't see it through the eyes of a child anymore. But I think that it moves quicker than before and that its life is richer in the summer heat. Because of the heat, its internal rhythm accelerates, and time shortens, the way it does for us when something oppresses us. I arrive at insane conclusions. Can one trust the mind? External conditions have their effect on one's mind as well. As a result, it is imperfect, a tool that submits to and modifies these external conditions, making everything doubtful, relative, unstable. Even the mind is a source of illusions. It sees and feels only that which its quality and constitution permit it to see and feel and nothing else. Oh, what an exile it is on this glowing, warm, and tender grass, where others peacefully slumber!

Doubt. A thousand-watt X-ray. A terrifying, penetrating force. Illusions fall deep within me, at the most extreme corners of my soul. You can see the bones and wounds. All of the vanities appear. And I understand that it's foolhardy to live beyond a certain age. We try to heal, to rectify our errors, and to mend our vices. And yet the elements destroy us nonetheless. We lose our wings, and we make more and more mistakes. And we find ourselves confronted by new and unknown vices. Life is bloody. A young man's recklessness is nothing compared with the daily struggle of a grown man. It's easy to be a hero when one has the enthusiasm for it and to be a saint when one's faith is strong. The real daredevil and conqueror is the person who rises against himself in his own solitude, from under the gaze of a death whose promises seem doubtful, and who pulls himself out of the dregs and the abyss of despair that his weariness has led him to, past the vain hope of respite and the fear of the viciousness that surrounds him, past his disgust at both himself and others and his own despair and arrogance, born from the knowledge of his own misery. Whoever retains the foundations of his own crumbling soul has also destroyed them, the wayward being who is ashamed of his own cowardice, both persecuted and persecutor. But once again, the rays of doubt transfix him. This recklessness is a form of impotence. Am I not exactly like the young boy who whistles in the dark so as to seem brave both to himself and to others? A simple lack of resolve?

And when my mind holds me in a vise and squeezes me like a spider, I envy the babies asleep in their carriages, and I am upset by them as well.

Is this inability to speak a lone, divine gift? Sometimes I remain this way for several days. I try to forget my emotion by throwing myself into my work. I decide to become an ordinary worker like the others. They are freer than I am. But my thoughts slip away on the fan belt of the whirring machine. They wrap themselves around my fingers. They go up and down on the pulleys and then onto the insufferable din created by the Linotype as if the latter were a ball held aloft above a jet of water. They are present like Hamlet's ghost. What is the use of living, as long as our sorrows aren't avenged and as long as we don't become what we'd imagined ourselves to be when we were young? I work like a robot as I think about my writings. It's a miracle that my fingers can compose without making a mistake. I hate machines. But all it takes is a few days without work, and I become disgusted by useless writings and books, by my futile meanderings and gossip. Then I return to my machine with joy, but a few days later, the bitterness returns. It even extends to my coworkers. I love them, yet I ignore them for days on end. I wish only happiness for those close to me, and yet I project my soul's darkness onto them. I poison their life. I poison my home, and I even poison my daily bread.

7

ANOTHER TRACT OF LAND. This one a wild, abandoned aviation strip. After each rain, a mud pond forms where children sometimes come to launch their small gliders. They barely make it off the ground before falling back down to earth, much like my enthusiasm. But where my gaze ends at the far edge of the field, the woods suddenly take on the majesty of mountains lost among clouds. An Ararat looking back at me. Emotion overtakes me in this deserted place, as it did along the shores in Moda at nightfall, where I went to observe my dreams ablaze on the Sea of Marmara, an avalanche of multicolored precious stones. But my gaze always stops on a thin cross that stands erect like a ruin amid this vague landscape. Suddenly, I become sad. Icarus, who had come years ago from the other side of the Atlantic to show us that man could fly, is buried here.

There was a crowd on that fateful day. The man leaving the airplane fluttered about left and right, up and down. Our admiration suddenly disappeared. And our cries couldn't retain him. And this horrible image of the crestfallen boy with golden hair has already disappeared. He lies there in that deserted place, already forgotten like the thousands of wartime soldiers, his only shroud the wings that envelop him. No one comes to lay flowers on his grave anymore. And the cross leans over to the right now, like my nostalgia for my homeland.

It requires courage to live past a certain age when you're no longer content with the word *destiny* and you don't find comfort anymore in the vain promises of an afterlife. You want to achieve all of the potential that you see in yourself. A thirst for victory, a stubborn desire to give meaning to an absurd life. And after being upset for days on end, I feel indignation at having let myself become upset. In the woods, my defeat becomes a victory, a resolution to move forward at all costs, a consequence of conflict with my fellow man. You gauge others, judge them, and then you reject them outright. Greatness becomes the search to find one's balance when faced with the abyss of disgust. A vengeance that slowly ferments. And so when I encounter a tree, I am filled with the mystery that emanates from it. At nightfall, the tree resembles that large mythical bird who wanted to capture the body and soul of the man he carried on his back and lead him into the light. The leaves sparkle like bursts of light on metallic feathers. The branches undulate like waves, as thin rays of light slide in between them. The battle between life and death fills me with the feeling that I am witnessing something truly extraordinary. And the cars' constant racket recalls another myth in which a boulder keeps falling back down each time the hero pushes it all the way up to the top of the mountain. I feel my shoulder's strength, made to carry this heavy load, and I also feel my weariness and my despair, as well as my stubborn willpower. I have the strength within me to keep writing as my pages transform themselves daily, as my gold turns to sand, and when, recoiling from myself and some manipulative demon, I join all of the critics who dislike my writing. I long for my real pages.

It's impossible to let go of the boulder. It's impossible to retreat. The village idiot is always happiest in his blind ignorance. After you've progressed so far, you can't return to the deceivers and the ignoramuses and accept the self-contentment of imbeciles. And I find myself looking down at them,

I who expect so much from their love, from their goodness, and from their praise. This man who waits, this beggar, I despise him as well. I accept the destiny of the person who, as he gets to know himself better, becomes all the more incomprehensible to others. And I also accept the tragedy of the person who distances himself by destroying all of his illusions, until he becomes a stranger even to himself. When confronted with truth, we feel useless to others and to ourselves; and truth is useless when we're alone in perceiving it. But daring makes life more beautiful, taking it beyond deceit at the price of solitude, suffering, and being rejected by others. My despair increases until it becomes hope and then finally pride.

8

THE BOIS DE VINCENNES extends beyond its own limits, one section after another, until it reaches the end of the city that lent it its name. In these parts of the forest, migrating birds help isolated trees and flowers to grow and communicate with one another. Each spring, they deliver a velvet pollen that comes to life amid the gravel and the rooftops, on the paws of a porcelain cat, or between the lips of the statue of a naked woman. And each fall, the woods cover them all with cotton-like flakes. A dream that holds dominion over the sky, after the cranes have flown by, as if their lamentations and loud croaking had transformed themselves into silk filaments floating in the air. And the same trees on which wolves sharpened their teeth and claws only a hundred years ago emit the sweetest perfumes. Acacia trees scatter their scents and the sweet perfume of fragrant women, while a heavy, hot odor arises from the tender grass. In the springtime, this air burns, voluptuous with the smell of the sea. Cars drive by and crush the flowers that cover the pavement. And the air doesn't resonate the way it does in winter, when the trees are like black metal. Now it resembles the air in an overcrowded room. You hear everything, as if it were all happening next door. Birds that flutter in the air, a flower that explodes, sap that overflows, a dew drop that slides away. In autumn, the air smells like a cave and a half-eaten watermelon, something that emerges from the past . . .

9

ON FOGGY DAYS, the Bois de Vincennes sometimes fills with a humid vapor and a bitterness that oozes from the trees' roots. And at times like these, the woods are a castle of dreams. The trees become shadows. They reach up to the sky and stretch to infinity. And the sky lowers itself, and one can hear everything within it: whisperings and footsteps, at times a falling tear, at others a beating breast. And in this invisible multitude, one also remains invisible to oneself. Oblivion. One finds oneself going beyond appearances and near everything that inhabits them. At the bottom of an ocean full of souls. The passing cars make the air tremble like the fluttering of angels' wings, and their lights are bells engulfed by the sea, the eyes of extraterrestrial beings . . .

It was on a day like this that I suddenly found myself standing in front of a statue. I had been walking down dark paths, observing the rare people who walked by like blind men, as car lights flickered hesitatingly in the fog. And I thought that life itself was like a fog, the same fog that fills human souls. I passed by the part of the forest where centuries ago, a messenger of goodness had suddenly developed a utopian doctrine that was meant to save the world. I felt sorry for him and wondered if it was really possible to be that naïve. He was a philosopher, a writer, and a musician, and he thought that man was naturally good. He was searching for man's happiness and thought that he could find it by going back to nature. And I felt that my reasoning was correct: human thought was only in its initial, confused stages. And suddenly, the statue. Steam rose from its gigantic pedestal, which was marked with barely visible inscriptions. And Beethoven was like an apparition aboveground. One could barely see his head, just a powerful bust turned to granite by the fog. A chest. And the phantom leaves swirling about placed a heart inside this stone. I saw him as if I were inside his music and even more deeply within his silent suffering. He'd created the most beautiful music. He had transformed his inner turmoil into a magical beauty; through his own suffering, he had consoled afflicted souls. But there was also a silence within him that he could never express, an anxiety that he alone could feel.

And everything inside him was bitter and despairing. All of his music was but the echo of this silence, the human part of the secret and enigmatic essence of his universal music. He was sad but also happy when this sadness consoled him. God gave him comfort. Love and art comforted him as well. His interpretation of man's virtues also comforted him, as did the fog and the beating of his heart and his faith in himself.

I was miserable in his company. The impossible, that very thing that transformed him into a genius, threw me into a panic and transformed me into a walking zombie. And the peace that I found in this fog was harmful and negative. Because, in fact, I felt a huge relief or, more precisely, a feeling of disgust toward this destroyed, tarnished world in ruins, lost in smoke. I felt disgust as well toward the scattering and darkening of my own soul. My solace was a crazed thing, an agitation of this rootless soul, of my veins, wetter still than the water-dipped branches that melt and disappeared drop by drop into the fog. Knowledge destroys the very thing that it enlightens.

10

ON RAINY DAYS, the same hesitation. In the summertime, the woods are beautiful beneath the rain. The scents and colors answer one another, as do invisible substances, bringing with them a new sensation. Each tree is a fountain. The rustling of trees and babbling of brooks melt into one another. The clouds glide, trees above the trees. The sun pokes through empty spaces, lighting up a branch or a bush here and there, or half a bench, a patch of grass, a moss-covered stone. And the cleansed greenery sparkles in the enveloping penumbra. In the shadowy part of the sky, a lightning bolt, like a javelin in flight, strikes the top of a tree, twisting it out of shape. And the tree shakes off this flame; after a brief struggle, it screams its anger with a monstrous trembling, its eyes fixed on the clouds that speed in its direction like a thousand ghosts. The earth trembles, and in the silence, light rays jump from blade to blade and leaf to leaf, while sounds echo down the forest paths that the wind creates as it loses itself within. The green crystals resonate and then quiet down. A fresh breeze passes through the hot, stuffy, woolen air.

It chases away a vaporous odor, a deluge of perfume emanating from the heart of the trees and the earth that reaches all the way up to my knees. The rain makes its way down a black asphalt road, and in certain spots, it reflects back a red sky underneath bouncing, boiling needles that magnetically echo off one another and shine and pierce my soul from all sides . . .

There was a time when I loved this rain. Now I see in it a battle that takes place beyond that which can be seen or felt. Intrigues, arguments, dramas, loves, and even the murder of invisible beings. One must be insane to settle for surface beauty and attract the gaze of invisible forces above us when one knows that they have no idea that we even exist. And here again, the pain that one feels when confronted with the impossible and the need to embellish our mistakes. The misery of man-homunculus.

I am still saddened after a storm when I encounter a fallen tree. One summer, I discovered both the good and the bad things that hailstorms can bring. Diamonds on the ends of branches, bees, honey drops that refused to melt in spite of the scorching heat. But little by little, the branches sagged under their weight, broke and tore apart like cloth, sometimes dragging bark along with them and exposing the tree's nakedness on their way down.

I liked the rainstorms when the clouds with their panther-like paws would pass above the trees and the wind would descend on them in a fury; when the branches would be crushed, trampled, torn, and shredded, as the leaves fell to the ground. I liked the sun's blazing sphere which lit up this storm like an evil eye.

A love of the red and troubled sea. A nostalgia for accidents and danger. At the age of ten, I already dreamed of thunder crashing down into my room, although a moment later, I would convince myself that I was the least adventurous child in the world. I liked danger when it remained at bay. Unconsciously, mischievously. How many times did I dream of a train flying off a bridge? And to think that at the time, people thought I was noble. I needed to appear superior and victorious like all of those petty tyrants who glorify in the slaughter of men, like paper tigers. A few real storms have brought me back to my senses and chased away my crazy presumptuousness, as well as the storm's imagined beauty.

Rain falls like a summer blessing, at times happy, at others sad. The sweet, wet wind seeps through my skin's every pore. And the light that emanates from the earth and the trees and the stagnant water illuminates me and makes me transparent. The rain resembles a grazing herd. But where might I go to find that dream again, the same gentle raindrops that fell upon me when I was a child? Oppressive reality remains inside me at all times now, and I understand the misery of a man caught walking in the rain. Paris had just fallen. I remember a pack of lost, starved dogs that I saw roaming in this forest without any master. They had given up on humanity and once again become wild. I saw them struggle under the driving rain, dazed, wandering about aimlessly. A few days later, I saw some of their scattered corpses.

One day, I saw the most magnificent rainbow stretched above the woods, a gigantic flower whose bright colors shone against the wet trees as a blazing car window went roaring by like a shooting star. A crystal prism of ever-changing colors. Behind the trees, the stained-glass windows of a church. But never before had I felt so deeply the futility of peace. So many more wars at the end of the rainbow . . .

And the rainbow troubled me until I remembered that it had spoiled my childhood.

I saw the illusions behind the history of nations, behind their tales and legends. Everything that shines above a nation like rainbows in the sky. Everything that repeats itself and multiplies, excites one's imagination, and makes one believe in some fantastic future. I saw the enormous bridge of light that had been built over the abyss linking one generation to another, as in a dream. And here the rainbow elicited another emotion in me. And I was afraid of the light, of a sacrilege for which I would never be forgiven.

In the rainbow's seven colors, I saw the seven deadly sins. And I understood that these sins made life what it was. Seven power plants that emitted their electricity in order to illuminate us. Art in particular owed them its enchanting beauty. And at the very moment when I refused to be deceived, standing in front of a lake that reflected back the rainbow, I remembered a book that I had once read in which the seven deadly sins were represented by seven sea monsters. And because I was convinced that it would be wrong to avoid them, that instead you had to fight them, they became even more daunting foes. Guile was a seven-tentacled monster that wore the face of a beautiful woman and carried in its hair and around its angelic neck countless vipers, worms, and spiders which started to move each time the monster raised its head as it slithered along the ocean floor on a long red crystal staircase. In this book, the brave hero's spear killed the monster, and the blood gushing from its injured neck oozed across the sea while smoke poured from its fallen, ivory head. But this death seemed unreal to me, because there wasn't a single virtuous person on earth who could defeat this monster. And also because we needed this monster in order to live and die by the grace of its magic. One of its venomous tentacles ended in a beautiful hand, fine and transparent, which floated beneath the waves' embraces, like a dream being born, a caress.

I was walking, pulling my shadow along the emeralds that hung on the tips of each stalk of grass, the diamonds that clung to each hyacinth, and once in a while, a tear would fall from one of the trees and land on my head.

11

DEEP INSIDE the Bois de Vincennes lies a small restless, ever-flowing waterfall. Whenever I go there, the face of a passport-office worker I once met comes back to haunt me. He had a bloody nose and didn't realize at the time that the simple "No" he uttered would unleash a storm within my young head. And this man with a bloodstained mustache and glasses saw a red flag when he looked at this adolescent, who seemed suspect because he was wearing a soldier's uniform which he'd dirtied sleeping outdoors and in train stations. A deserter perhaps? Red also was the notebook in which he wrote a list of strange names as he cursed out loud. Foreigners, cowards all of them!

The cannons thundered in the distance. The office worker was embarrassed. He signed his name, gave the boy his passport, asked him his nationality, and, surprised, furrowed his brow. "Kharasho . . ."

The boy angered easily. One day, in a different country, he shocked yet another officer in a military prison. He could never forgive the man who had slapped him across the face. He demanded to be set free and screamed his innocence at the top of his lungs. He carried within him the horror of the dead bodies he had seen, and he protested in the very name of civilization. His words were passionate, spontaneous, rhetorical. Later on, formal education would do away with all of this passion, and the deception that followed would surpass the emptiness of his words. Deception leads to a type of silent courage. But where to? . . .

In the summer, dusk lends a particular beauty to this wild part of the woods, where the earth appears wedged between endless waves of green. Water flows into a nearby lake. Waves slide by like transparent serpent heads, supple and crystalline in the fading sunlight. The water level rises and falls like a man's chest, uniting, mirror-like, the sky and the images of the surrounding trees. Worms twist and turn beneath the foam. On the shore, a leaf left over from the previous autumn watches, ashen and fine like a woman's silk embroidery. Worn thin by the hands of time, the falling rain, and the snow, reduced only to the outline of its veins: beautiful.

The tops of the cypress trees touch one another high above the ground. In their arms, silence is a young doe. Love is fresh and sacred here, like a Persian miniature. One senses the presence of a young girl who once appeared and then disappeared just as suddenly under these branches, a young girl who joined the others who came before her, each one carrying a promise within her and each one creating a heaven where they would welcome me after my death.

A stream separates the trees that face one another on either shore like a wedding procession. They wait, clothed in multicolored silk. Light green holds dominion like an urgent cry. A royal groom who sometimes throws his luminescent bridle to the princess of the Alans, who waits on the opposite shore. The princess's heart beats wildly, and her honey-colored hair glows. Pearls, emeralds, and diamonds rain down from the sky. The leaves are diaphanous, simple, and fresh. Some are as richly colored as peacock feathers, while others give off the same dark violet hue as ripe blackberries, and still others have been dyed with henna. Some are silver and shudder between heaven and earth, held together by filaments of light. Others tremble like the throats of doves, while still others flutter like butterfly wings. And when the sky turns red behind them and the sun smiles like a golden Buddha from behind endless columns of light, happiness reigns, an odd bliss that emanates from an enormous, strange temple. Exiled, birds rush toward the light. As if captured in an invisible net, they fly anguished, opening and closing their squawking beaks until they finally shake off the magnetic and poisonous gaze of the greenery below from their outstretched wings.

My happiness quickly turns to melancholy. I'm sad for all of the beautiful things that will never return, for everything that fades, for lost sunsets, and especially for that one last twilight after which I will never see or feel anything again . . .

I'm sad because my being remains divided between flesh and ecstasy. I'm sad when I come upon a tree whose bark shines like a naked woman and whose leaves, when they burn, fly away and are reduced to the good and the sublime. In this light, at the height of love itself, I understand that love is only a physical passion and that our first attraction results from a woman's outer beauty. This beauty is at the heart of all vices. As our forefathers understood, it is neither good nor evil. But a weak being, inept when confronted by ecstasy or by creation itself, still charms and troubles us to the core, sometimes offering itself up to us and sometimes not, sometimes depriving us of its soul after we have already penetrated deep inside it, and sometimes abandoning itself to us, while closing off all of its doors.

I remain divided. Is it her flesh or her soul that emanates from within her? A passion that sometimes demands satisfaction, relentless and scornful. And sometimes I feel nostalgic, as in adolescence, with the desire to turn beauty into a goddess, to renounce all earthly pleasures for something more exalted. I am cut in half by this century. Where are all of the noble women? All of the ones surrounding us just chase after money and physical pleasure.

In this red hallway, my being remains divided between God and his creatures, between matter and thought, and before the mystery that we call God. We implore him from the depths of our suffering, and yet he does not answer. Sometimes we beg, sometimes we protest against sin, and life remains incomprehensible. Sometimes we reject him as we reject the origin of our ignorance. Sometimes we accept his existence the same way we accept the infinite, which ignores us completely. This religion, which creates mystery in proportion to man's egotism, has no effect on me, in spite of the fact that my entire being yearns for ecstatic transcendence.

And I remain divided in the twilight that lifts me above myself, near the waterfall where the light shines forth from a life's worth of readings. It blazes forth like a mirror's cry. It gushes, falls back onto the artificial rocks, and rains down, sowing its diamonds like a colt that shakes its wings of light. And the crystals ride on the wind, each one a magic sword. The waters ring like gold coins thrown down by David of Sassoon. A great love of life. But also great disappointment. An Orpheus who witnessed his dream turned to stone as he returned from hell.

And I remain divided between myself as a boy and as an old man. What is blind enthusiasm really worth, and what is clairvoyance in turn worth, if it kills all enthusiasm? A drama.

12

BEHIND THE WATERFALL lies a long, tree-lined mirror. Its water is thick and stagnant. The water continues to sleep as mosquitoes glide along its surface, forming thin concentric rings. And then I discover the mediocrity of self-satisfied people who have no bitterness within them. But am I being fair to them? The cascade owes its existence to such waters. I should have liked all of these mediocrities, I should have pardoned them and respected them because, in point of fact, we are created by them. To hear, to see, to compare, and to find in all of this one's personality and even to write books thanks to these mediocrities. But who can guarantee that there's any wisdom in doing so? How can we know what we take from the world outside us and what comes from within? Who can assure me that all of this is just and authentic and not corrupt instead? Who will appease me amid all my wealth that I cannot believe in yet will not abandon? I understand the monster in the fable who chewed on his own flesh in order to live and to be able to continue gnawing at himself. I would have thrown away these treasures, I would have retired to some dark cave, if I couldn't discern an illusion even in our denials. Who will appease me when faced with mediocrity, when the conflict between pity and disdain leaves me no options?

The cascade gushes. Its water grumbles. All of my thoughts arrive with their own preexisting contradictions. My bitterness is happiness, my despair hope, my disgust compassion, my compassion a sham. And my joy grows into sadness and my sadness into joy. Sometimes from tree to tree, from one tree to another, my gaze seeks something out. Tossed about, the treetops give off light. What is this sunlight that satisfies, troubles, and intoxicates me, the beauty of this rustling and the movement of a thousand palms? What a glorious summer! What a glorious sky, filled with marble statues of the gods erected in order to bring to life all of our potential greatness. So many opportunities to transform our inanities into a celestial language. Our stubborn ignorance kills everything born of fire and sea. What is this ecstasy that comes from music, that inebriates and troubles me so? And what of love? Even its wound is sweet. Love that I still passionately await, even after it has cut into me, down to the very marrow in my bones? And what of all of the hypocrisy that we pull off with a straight face? Waves of silence break over us. The clouds bleed. And side-by-side, the trees straighten up as if to sing, only to separate again in the darkness. Trumpets blare. Divine heaven, filled with women as good as Mary, mother of God, intoxicating like the water jet on which our heart turns, bathed in light, regal as a lion. And it is woman, through her love and sublime devotion, who leads us to transcendence. And yet the sun's rays slowly diminish. The candles blow out. The marble wears thin. And one hears the sound of the heavy funeral march: darkness, my thoughts.

It will go on like this until our death. Waiting followed by deception. And what is truly tragic is that this waiting seems neither vain nor meaningless. It is the way things should be. The results of our centuries-old meditations are tawdry, and the inebriation of our senses are ephemeral when compared with our suffering. Yet from thought to sensation and from sensation to thought, from bitterness to joy, we are in perpetual movement. We always lie in wait, and yet everything that we await simply comes and passes. Insatiable. Ever searching. Dissatisfaction, which leads to satisfaction.

Even despair is a source of hope, perhaps a more important one than faith. Only in despair can we begin to understand that we must be above hope and faith, things that only the weak cling to. Only the weak hope and believe—it's easy to believe and to hope. What is truly difficult is to carry despair and doubt within oneself: these are the things that frighten men. A woman wants a man who is sure of himself and inspires confidence in her. A student becomes a master's disciple when he answers his questions with confidence. And the masses always turn to leaders who are strong in their convictions and in the truths they espouse. And all of the wars, conflicts, and disasters spring from this one weakness, from the ease and desire that people have to believe in something. The same is true of all affairs of the heart. Because, in essence, faith becomes a dream, a fiction, a naiveté that profits all those who know how to exploit it. It's because of faith that nations and religions, political parties as well as individuals, clash, and it's because of faith that they persecute and destroy one an other. And yet if people only learned to question things more often, they would learn that no one has the right to claim exclusive access to truth and to destroy what others consider sacred. There are many truths, and no truth is final. When will fanaticism give way to doubt, to its goodness and wisdom, so that war might end and the world know peace? When will conceited and pretentious writers and their stupid followers have the courage to recognize the virtue of skepticism, so that a real, authentic art may finally lead them to victory? When will these pontificators finally hold their tongues and understand the moral bankruptcy of claiming victory with words and promises as old as the hills, which have been broken one after another since the dawn of time and ultimately aborted?

Will they ever comprehend the anguished beauty of that dawn, of the moment when the birds escape from the serpent's green gaze? My despair is the very source of my hope. In this I resemble a tree that derives its strength from the waste of its own discarded leaves.

Doubt is a heavenly poison created so that man will not be poisoned. It even neutralizes its own poison. By throwing us into a state of desperation, it gives us the strength to doubt our own despair. It makes us good when confronted with evil and evil when confronted with good. And when these two forces do battle within us, we discover divine grace. Doubt is the very core of our wisdom. The birth of good and evil.

I was born with it and grew up in its midst. I always doubted the lessons they taught us in school. I doubted whether the train would ever leave the station. I doubted whether I had locked the door when I left my house. I questioned whether the metro headed to Porte Maillot might take me instead in the opposite direction to Porte Champerret. Or that the tunnel walls weren't about to close in and trap the subway car deep within the earth's bowels. I didn't have an ounce of confidence in architects. Here's another word that tired souls can't stop using: *confidence*. Now, there's a sin that hangs over our people. I had every diploma known to man, yet I was afraid that I would be refused a work permit. I was afraid that a police officer would arrest me and imprison me without reason. I had barely finished paying for a cup of coffee, yet I was afraid that the waiter would come chasing after me. What a low opinion I had of men! My first inkling of them came through fables, from the breath of demons. Then came the wars and a revolution, leaving cadavers and ruins in their wake. Then came our national history. Then love. What haven't I tried in order to deal with my anxiety and to transform this illness into a philosopher's stone of goodness? And thanks to love, once again to find innocent souls in these murky waters and finally to understand the suffering that most men experience. Thanks to her, I quickly forget the pain that comes from being judged by other men, and I immediately forget the jubilation that comes with praise. Thanks to her as well, I feel nostalgic for goodness. Those who carry evil in their hearts do so unconsciously, or else they are living by nature's laws. There are truths that have nothing truthful about them. Deceitful values, white lies that we sometimes tell out of kindness, as we do when we are in love.

And this doubt seems to me to be a virtue. And yet I know that we only reach our goals by pursuing them steadfastly. I also know the degree to which we can be unpleasant, negative, and destructive when we mistrust our friends. Then we can become truly abominable, especially with loved ones. There's a pettiness in all pretentious swagger, a lack of forethought and intuition. A shamelessness. Hence I could never make a speech. I could stop a random person on the street, but I could never get him to believe any of my brilliant ideas. Doubt is a psychological disorder within which the purification and crystallization of the soul occurs. It forms a person by making all appearances transparent to him. Doubt is a force when it has experienced destructive love and left behind all of the other sickening hesitations and replaced them with a realistic, clear vision of the world, once all illusions have crumbled. When a woman, for instance, has defied her lover only to destroy him later on. I've met such women. I had a friend whose kindness, strength, and enthusiasm came entirely from knowing such a woman. And to him, she seemed happy and satisfied, as long as he sacrificed everything for her happiness. My friend woke up one bright morning fooled by his own satisfaction, complaining that he no longer doubted anything. He understood the insanity of pleasure. Yet he had never really known the woman he loved, not even her body as it exploded with pleasure. He was ashamed that she had deceived him. His eyes learned to search her out, and his newfound doubt became a source of wisdom.

I noticed a similar awakening in another friend of mine. He fell from his egotistical pedestal and lost his self-confidence. His pride collapsed. Jealousy. Stupefaction. Indignation at the very moment that his eyes filled with tears. A relentless desire to reclaim his lost love. So many contradictions! A litany of insults. The separation led to delirium, then a fall. His hands trembled to touch and not to touch this beautiful woman who was rejecting him. He loathed this race to which he didn't belong. He banished this foreign woman's flesh from his own, and yet he would bury himself in her. He fought to free himself as he would from the murky current that was dragging him under. He cursed the carnal desire that led him to this foreign woman who had betrayed him yet made him grab on to her. He felt his heart's true love more deeply now that their bodies were separated. But this separation, the death of love, was painful beyond reckoning.

He was battling himself at the very moment when his life had become most painfully intense. He felt every possible romantic emotion gushing from his heart. But pride put an end to those waves of emotion that would lead to slavery and annihilation. A battle: his arms trembled to embrace or not to embrace her. He tried to analyze his situation, and little by little, he recognized the first signs of love's hypocrisy hiding behind insignificant words and events. He relived the entire past, the year gone by, which he had shared with this woman who was abandoning him now. He spoke to her, he gave her proof of his sincerity and of his love for her, only to end up terrorized and tortured when faced with this sphinx who was receding before him. He was ashamed of his suffering and of his misery. He had become a mass of flesh unable to talk or think, reduced to delirium by the sweetness of a past that would never return.

I took him in my arms after his lover had left him. An unforgettable night. Snow was falling outside and, along with it, silence. What could I possibly say to console him? I felt as if his soul were falling apart, tattered. He was alone in a strange and far-off land, on a planet that man had abandoned, a place my words could not reach. His voice came to me from the bottom of his soul: "She was my entire world." And I knew that it was useless to heap insults upon this most detestable woman, she who had also made this man kind, proud, and self-confident.

A few years later, I saw his face again, and now it moved me beyond words. It was kind and noble in a way known only to souls who have encountered vanity and thus begun to doubt everything. Now this face was at peace. It carried with it the peacefulness of a man who has become his own master.

Everything holy becomes sullied. All noble beauties become revolting. And only the heart that has suffered such things becomes truly wise.

13

I LOVE THE PART of the woods where the waterfall lies. I cross the footbridge, which took me almost twenty years to name: the Skeptic's Bridge. And even this name isn't truly appropriate, because my mind hasn't been able to control my desires. Often an urge overcomes me to hold a beautiful face in my hands. Because a skeptic knows how to stop when faced with danger. He also knows how to suppress his doubts and remain strong. All things that I'm incapable of doing, although they form an important part of my illusions. I can't submit to any wisdom. My enthusiasm wanes as quickly as it rises. I refuse to bow down to reason when reason terrorizes men's souls. I also refuse to give in to reason when it is too quick to bear its own heavy burden. Intelligence should rise above all of these considerations. But when I stop on the bridge, I understand that one shouldn't form any earthly attachments. Everything constantly changes, including people. The bridge moves, and I feel an urge to sing as I did when I was a child, when I used to watch the road go speeding by from a car or when I used to watch waves hit and slide away against the side of a boat. My desire to cross over is ancient. Now I'm tired of all of society's values, which inevitably come to an end and then change. And at times, something sweet:

> *Passent les jours et passent les semaines,*
> *Ni temps passé*
> *Ni les amours reviennent*
> *Sous le pont Mirabeau coule la Seine.*[1]

Far away, behind the trees, the sound of metal balls as they roll by and clang against one another. The idle, the young, and the old play like children. They argue, then measure the distance that separates the balls. Farther on, behind tables where others play cards, the children's carousel turns, round and round. Through the branches, wooden swans and horses appear and disappear. Generations pass by. The wheel's rotations make the sunlight flicker. Shadows break apart and embrace again. In the distance, the languorous tones of a primitive music also separate and come back together again, as if they had emerged from a childhood world.

> *L'amour s'en va comme cette eau courante,*
> *L'amour s'en va*
> *Comme la vie est lente.*[2]

14

FARTHER DOWN in the woods lies a small lake. In the middle of this lake, cypress trees point toward the sky. I remember our cemeteries. Sometimes my soul rises up to these treetops, where the air is as pure and honest as in a dream. At the bottom, behind some heavy, impenetrable ivy shrubs, a chicken coop reminds me of the one we had growing up in my father's house.

---

1   From Guillaume Apollinaire's "*Le Pont Mirabeau.*"

2   Ibid.

What did I love so much about chickens and barns when I was a child, and why would I get so upset at night at the thought of all of those animals that had been left alone in the dark? Why do these feelings from so long ago seem like a lost idyll now that my hair has begun to turn white, and why do I still become emotional at nightfall when the ducks and the chickens return to their henhouses? A few tufted willows, disheveled and genuflecting in mid-lake, make me shudder, sadder and more melancholic yet. Greenery covers the water's surface so that sometimes it becomes a field, an emerald carpet that you would like to step out onto. Sometimes it becomes a black mirror. Honey under moonlit clarity, sponge-like and soft, like medusas when the wind hits. The swarming of a thousand worms, leading all the way to the lights from a nearby dance. And under their silken threads, the blazing eyes of a few houris. The ones I danced with long ago, when I still knew how to dance, and those I've forgotten as well. Jeanne, Suzanne, Colette, and others whose names I've also forgotten. Like all young people who believe youth to be eternal, do they mock my newfound marital bliss, as they waste their lives away? Jeanne, Suzanne, Colette, and other emancipated women, stupidly proud of your bodies, of your beauty, of your coquettishness, rockets that appeared at the threshold of my youth. Girls who bloomed after the First World War with the international armies, back in the days when life became intoxicated by victory and dissipation. Desperate girls, tired by centuries of wars, by religion, by chastity belts, girls from a frenetic civilization whose sole ambition was simply to enjoy life, to know pleasure, and to go on, intoxicated. Girls of superficial pleasures. All your love of men was simply a pleasant duel. You were seduced by sweet words, by flowers, by money. You liked men who pretended to be servile in order to cheat on you, men who toadied up to you, who smiled, who gave in to you, or else men who stalked you with an obstinate and obscene desire. Jeanne, Suzanne, Colette, and others, slaves to your own liberation. The unemancipated women in my country were much happier. You are the daughters of a century whose symbol is sex appeal. Women were getting undressed everywhere: onstage, in hotels, on beaches, in front of the basin at the water spouts. Beauty was an easy weapon for actresses. The talent was in their legs, their eyebrows, and their breasts. Jeanne, Suzanne, Colette, and others who knew that before anything else, it was their legs by which they were judged. Girls of a materialistic century without morals, you loved by scorning love itself, and you became inebriated while despising anything spiritual. And the timid lover's trance as he makes the mistake of wanting to remain above all mistakes, keeping inside you for your old age the love stories of the past, the romantic dreams where you pondered your own downfalls. You lived and grew old, perhaps without understanding that women are victims, deceived whichever way they turn, and without understanding that you had been deprived of great beauty, despite your freewheeling ways. Or perhaps you found all of this behavior natural. But maybe that's what love is: pitiful . . .

These days, I spend sad twilights and nights by the lake. Existence is a calculus. The lost years disturb me, as they disturbed Faust as well. A desire to fill the void left behind by books. The thirst for beauty, when beauty has already grown ugly and when beauty has already become truth in our minds. A concentrated effort to forget the absurdity of living. The pain of not being able to take on any identity besides a narcissistic one. A Narcissus who suffers from the fact that his image continues to change. Insanity: the stubborn desire to continue writing under conditions that offer absolutely no rewards. Our language, on the verge of dying out. Our values, denied by strangers, by the diaspora, and even by our own homeland, where art is forced to be both hypocritical and simplistic. Part of our people—the diaspora—stands on the verge of being assimilated, while another part is condemned to assimilation in its own country. And when you're abroad, you assimilate more while keeping this country and your intense love for it within you. So you assimilate, ashamed, all the while being aware of the foolishness of a reality that only hides your inner emptiness.

So I stay and watch the swans glide by in the dark, and sometimes I imagine the greatness of centuries gone by, in the calm trees now plunged into obscurity, from whose branches stars appear to hang down. The swans glide by, savage and proud. They shine in the light, marble white. They pass in the shadows, while the crystals troubled by the mystery of their passing wake tremble like branches, transforming these mysterious rays that appear out of nowhere into stars. And occasionally, the waves caress the floating moon's chest and kiss the rocks and the earth that line the riverbanks with their crazed and unappeased desire. They arrive in the warm nighttime, like the dreams of a naked, lascivious woman, prostrate and proud in her radiant beauty, like a veil fluttering in the air, like sparkling diamonds, while far away, the water flowing down from a ravine tells the story of all of the failed beauties in a low, anguished, and cruel voice. All happiness is really sadness in disguise. The lone tree on the riverbank stands silent and dreamy, like the Danish prince who sometimes spent his time staring at the lake in the royal garden in order to forget his troubles and find an excuse to uncover the deceit in his surroundings. And we hear his whisper, "To be or not to be." To write or not to write. . . . The waves arrive, carrying with them Ophelia's mourning, sad when confronted with the death of a virgin love. The waves also arrive like laughter. Hamlet laughs . . .

Sometimes I walk by the ballroom. A regret? The craziness of the dances and of the joy they gave was so painful. They killed in me the doctor I might have been, the one people respect in spite of his usurious greed. They also killed the artist in me, the Sorbonne graduate, the merchant, all of these nothings that pass for something. A hardship but a satisfaction as well. There's no light without a fire.

In the semiobscurity, hanging from the ceiling, a luminous globe still turns, its reflections vibrating like myriad butterflies. They glide above the dancers' heads, slowly turning, while from different angles in the room, the slender lights pour out their red and green songs like flutes. A false dream, a deception. Out of the head of a little glass imp, a hellish dream arises. A network of lights. Why does joy always make me sad as well? I watch. The same old tune plays to a different rhythm, sometimes laughing like a satyr, sometimes inspired like a Casanova flattering a woman, and sometimes groaning from the burning desire of a sex that suddenly roars and throws against the wall women's breasts that he's frenetically ripped out. The same crowd. A generation's gone by, but the tree continues to shudder. The same cauldron. The same boss who's going to empty the pockets of a few more generations, who's going to intoxicate and satisfy and indulge in a few more virgins, who'll fill and tame his stomach with the human grist that'll feed his mill. This human comedy—such drama—always claims the same victims. And my sweet memories darken when confronted with this constantly turning, moving, jumping, skipping pile of hysterical flesh. I feel these girls against my chest, each one with her own heat, her own perfume and suppleness. A wave pulls me under, alongside my dreams. A tree that I would have uprooted. And a desire for new caresses and new conquests, as if love were man's supreme accomplishment, even when he knows that it's all in vain. But my mind's shining globe sweeps this all aside.

I wander off and take the road that borders the woods, turning once again toward the lake, only to notice that it's lit up by the night lights of a passing car. The trees' shadows descend on the lake like persecuted souls. They hit one another, fall down, and get up again, stretch out and then shorten while couples appear here and there and dot the warm grass with their embraces. This light reminds me of the blanket that one of my friends pulled back one morning in order to show me his conquest, a beautiful naked Frenchwoman—his tenth, he claimed. One of the trees shines from all its whiteness. And then darkness suddenly falls. It falls like the earth that covered my unfortunate friend a few months later as he withered and passed away. And here comes another tree, a handsome criminal. And the darkness again. Another fallen friend. So many friends whom I met at dances closed their eyes for the last time on a hospital bed. Orphans saved from the deportations. Young men liberated from the prison that families represent. After being sexually frustrated where they came from in the Orient, they became sexually crazed in the West. Here they worked all day and danced all night, debauched themselves until dawn, and then ran off again to the factory after having slept only a few hours. And whenever I think of the victims we left behind, the lake beneath the light shining like metal, undulating like a cheap whore, seems like a memory from long ago that I don't have the courage to face. The trees on the island hang in the emptiness. Behind them, I notice a crazed lunatic appear with his electric gadgets and his murderous mirrors, while a priest who came from afar to bury a young boy stops, fixed in place, his lips cursing as he recites a prayer.

A car glides by like a diamond needle on a waxen record. It gallops behind the light that sinks to the bottom of the magic woods like a white castle. And I remember the imaginary castle that we always chased after but never reached, whose ivory doors always remained closed to us. A phantom running in the dark, slowly shrinking, a vibrant and dying vision, like a butterfly. It's the drama of a soul that doesn't want to submit to itself, of a mind that gives up the ability to make judgments and that doubts everything about everyone. A mind that agrees with everyone.

What a change since that day long ago, in these same woods, when I greeted civilization with open arms. Since then, I've seen promises slip away and glide over people's heads: the unreachable white castle that symbolizes freedom and beauty, brotherhood and joy. I saw progress go backward, slowly transformed into the most vile treachery. Diabolical.

Sometimes I walk slowly under the arched trees, as if I were afraid of the man I might become with each new step I take. I change with every waking moment until I become a stranger even to myself. Who am I? What nation and which country do I belong to? I turn away from the world, bitter. Unfortunately, I don't do so out of some praiseworthy revolt meant to preserve an identity that comes from my own people, even if I do carry deep within me the cruel destiny of that people. I'm all alone. My mind has made the mistake of reaching that place where all beliefs fall, like so many illusions and false idols. There comes a time of self-abnegation in one's life when one believes that one can build the most just and magnificent edifice. We take an entire lifetime in order to become this terrified architect who can't even find his way his way out of his own building. Who am I, who didn't inherit a single iota of my father's reverence or of my mother's faith? I am ashamed to open the Narek,[3] which my father would often read from at night. I'm ashamed to enter a church, fearing that I might have to feign religious sentiments that I don't possess. A desire overcomes me to fall to my knees and cry, and at the same time, pride overwhelms me, and I want to rail against and attack those people who are able to genuflect before God. Egotism and deception lie behind their prayers, whether or not they realize it. Even saints try to save their own souls. But what do I try to fall back on,

---

3   Sarafian refers here to the tenth-century volume of prayers titled *The Book of Lamentations* by Gregory Narekatsi. This book has attained a cult-like status among religious Armenians. Referred to simply as "the Narek," it has been blamed by Shahan Shahnour, among others, for the servile mind frame that Armenians have allegedly been victims of for the past thousand years.

if not the attempt to reconcile life's beauty and its absurdity, to try to find common ground between these men and myself, to save myself from oblivion through art, to take pleasure in kindness and love, in other words, finally to live? To pull myself together when I fall part, not to suffer when faced with death. Sometimes I lean toward the sensual, at others toward the intellectual. Sometimes I cling to transcendence, at others I think of transcendence as an illusion that only death will end. At times, I deny the existence of life after death, and I think that once we are dead, we won't even remember who we once were. Sometimes I cling to that treasure called reality, and I retreat into myself. Who created this reality, where I exist in such a chaotic state? A chaos that possesses harmony and order as well. There's morality, faith, mysticism, socialism, all things that might have melded together in a harmonious symphony if there had just been some power to bring them together and without which they continuously remain apart from one another. That's the mistake that the diaspora-born commits, between the fall of religion and the dawn of science, carrying with him doubtful origins, as well as the talent to adapt to any situation. What am I, born to several languages yet master of none, not even of my mother tongue, which I returned to after becoming a stranger to myself in a foreign school? What am I, who condemns my own people even though my entire outlook is conditioned by this people's suffering, which I place above all others? Only when I am far from my own people, in solitude, do I comprehend its full scope. I become its disciple, to the point where I can't get myself to speak a foreign language without cursing its practitioners and without wanting to preserve my own personality no matter what happens. What am I who becomes unsettled in front of any crowd that parades by yet feels ashamed to walk behind their banner and instead takes refuge behind my own idiosyncrasies? Born cosmopolitan by nature, I become nationalistic in the extreme. And when faced with the foreign mob, I forget nationalistic anger and suffering. I become heartless and deride all doctrines. What am I, who feels free in an ivory tower that others who lead a public life criticize? These people know nothing about the infinite, while I find myself constantly confronting it. These people are blind, prisoners of an illusory freedom, yet implacable and tyrannical in the name of liberty. Born into revolution, the intelligentsia's servility nauseates me.

They're all hired guns, as were the deportation guards. The pleasure they find in their work weighs on my conscience. And yet their betrayal is sweeter to the oppressed mob than the most sincere words that I utter and that remain incomprehensible to them, since they fall outside the purview of passion, of superficial judgments and loud enthusiasms. And I, who tell nothing but the truth, appear more false than the most treacherous rhetorician who speaks the language of deception. What am I, an intellectual or a worker? I feel comfortable with neither one nor the other. I am revolted by both yet look to each of them for salvation.

I love art, and I am ashamed by it. I love manual work, but I also love the leisurely life of the independently wealthy, traveling from one country to the next, and all of the advantages that money brings. I love all of these things yet know them all to be fleeting. An entire life sacrificed to the insanity of writing. Ever doubtful of divine salvation, suffering and then disowning my effusive enthusiasms from the day before, I despair at the sleaze that others wear on their faces because of their inexperience and their self-satisfaction, which becomes for them a kind of grace. An entire life dedicated to manual labor, where I've been subjected to the most humiliating impositions. My body and soul are weary. And when my better half's complaints quite rightly egg me on, stimulate and persecute me, my thoughts turn to becoming wealthy. Yet I know that my conscience would never forgive me if I did this, that I would be deprived of feeling and even of life and pleasure. I would go so far as to say that I would even be deprived of the pleasure that I derive from both art and work. I was born under the star of disgust.

A chaos born from the sin of intelligence, as are our century and its entire civilization.

15

THE BOIS DE VINCENNES is a windswept ocean at night. The waves ceaselessly unfurl. . . . They slide, bang into one another, froth, and foam as they crash against the darkness. A branch creaks like a mast. A bicycle light passes by like a pirate's lantern. Another one answers from deep within the woods, lighting up the night, black and wet, and shining like a waxen canvas. A ship glides by above trees plunged into darkness. The branches break and fall to the ground. But my anxiety is even greater when the woods are calm in the dark and the countless sphinxes remain silent. The majesty of it all horrifies me. A ferocious beast with velvet paws. I remember the thieves and the criminals who would rob anyone who walked through the woods and who sometimes left their naked corpses behind. I remember the prostitutes and the girls from good families who gave away their bodies behind bushes, in spite of the guards making their rounds. And when fear and bitterness torment me, I imagine a perfect civilization that could only be born of superior intelligence. Then intelligence wouldn't be a mask that we wear like a disguise and apply to a religion that preaches love and a philosophy that preaches materialism. We'd be more honest if we just admitted that we love ourselves above all else. And it's by loving ourselves more effectively that we'll also be able to act more fairly toward others. Such a culture would be based on individuality, rather than on communities that are devoid of any. Sooner or later, man will have to reach this perfect consciousness of his own identity. Every doctrine in the world opposes such a realization, because it wants to enslave man. Religion does this by inventing heaven and hell; others achieve the same end by building prisons and so-called industrial paradises. Man must be a man. That's what Zarathustra should have announced and left aside the serpent and the lion. Oh, intelligence! My bitter cup.

16

WHEN ANXIETY OVERCOMES ME, the woods' electric lights seem more splendid than diamonds. And the lights that illuminate the houses behind the trees are as beautiful as in dreams. Man's presence encourages me. I realized this once when I was extremely ill. I was at the bottom of an abyss. A vile being, spineless and faceless, too weak even to catch sight of the light above the abyss and understand the joy of those living above. Life is beautiful when we are about to lose it. We don't remember any of its misery or hardships. I cried so that I wouldn't die, although I constantly think of death as a deliverance and a purification when I am healthy. When I approach it, death seems horrifying, the incomprehensible mystery that lies behind disappearing without a trace. And the slight probability that immortality might exist becomes a nightmare. On that day, my senses and my thoughts abandoned me; I had become a tearful wreck. But a more lucid wreck, I thought, than the person who throws himself like some supposed hero into the abyss of death or the person who departs this world thinking that he will find a more just afterlife.

Contradictions haunt me wherever I go. I wanted to be strong, and here I am, weaker than the weakest man, simply because I'd like to place intelligence ahead of the tyranny that it exerts on myself and others. I used to be brave and daring. Now I've become a coward who sometimes suffers from his own cowardice and who's sometimes satisfied to revisit the folly of his past brazenness and the misery that all brave young people experience. Little by little, I regain my courage. Everything is unstable at the remotest limits of the human soul, where I've searched in vain for stability. An unending ocean.

The birth of a real ocean perhaps, on whose shores I was born one fine spring day, when even the air itself was overcome with anxiety. The bulls and the bells answered one another. The echoes from the waves reached my crib like a mother's call. My childhood knew many storms, waves that continually renew themselves. And the sea, black at times, was an immense bird at night, furiously beating its wild wings against the rocky shore, struggling ferociously to keep rising ever higher and in the process making the houses tremble all around. The sea was a calm and azure plain under a summer sun, a racetrack full of white horses. There at daybreak, angels did battle with demons. At night, the lights emanating from the ships docked in the harbor turned this plain into the most dazzling Christmas tree. I would watch the sea from the highest window in our house and imagine untold worlds and treasures. And one day, while I was still a child, I decided to follow my dreams. I was no longer satisfied with this small city, where several ethnicities bumped into one another, ours being the most miserable, I thought. And I'm still walking today, floating like a plant without roots. For far-away, beautiful things became ugly as they moved closer in and ugly things became beautiful as they moved far away. How happy I would be today to find myself among the poor people of my native city again, to see for even an instant the simple-minded teachers, the priests, the actors, and the revolutionaries, to see them again and to watch them go by, since my destiny is to keep on walking. Because I still remember the bird that beat the rocks with its giant wings and sometimes rose all the way to where the air grows thin. When he fell back down to earth and his heart exploded, he came back to life again from the blood he had shed.

17

IN THE BOIS DE VINCENNES, there are cicadas and trees from my native city. Sometimes I think I hear the whisperings that rocked my childhood cradle, flowing on a wave of gold and crystal. After the row boat, the village path was another boat with its countless shrubs and crickets. Holding my brother-in-law's hand, I would reach the top of the hill, leaving the sea below us. I felt close to the stars. My brother-in-law would wipe the sweat from his brow, and his jovial smile, the smile of a happy man, made me feel for the first time the existence of what we call a soul. Sometimes deep inside the woods, I lie down and try to recall those faces from the past, and I try to hear the silvery vibrations of the myriad insects that touched my childhood. Butterflies tremble as they shatter the sun's rays. And around me, everything is in motion on the ground, in the grass and in the bushes, under the trees'

bark and underneath the moss. Ants, beetles, flies—insects of all kinds. And
now I slowly find myself at one with them and with the earth, the rocks, the
trees, and the sun's vibrating rays. I feel the unity of all living things, that
same feeling that led us to the idea of monotheism. What changes must have
occurred, what events unfolded, in order to make lifeless, primordial matter
divide into a million different shapes and become imbued with the mystery
of life, to take the form of a tree, a rock, a man, or an animal? And I relive
the evolution of man and his thoughts, from the beginning of time until the
very moment when my brother-in-law wiped the sweat from his brow. For
this miracle is also a tragedy. And in the Bois de Vincennes near Charenton,
there is a whiff of this most terrible spiritual tragedy. It comes from a mouth
that has sung of maidens of fire and abstract hells in countless nightmares.
A noble poet who finally hanged himself one night from a lamp post of the
great city. Lucidity is the greatest danger: it must be overcome by logical
thought, and one must maintain a child's innocence in the process.

Miserable and exhausted, I am overtaken by the desire to fall asleep
deep within the woods. To forget everything. Not to feel the weakness of my
body and mind. But what would be the point of sleeping? Tense, nervous,
irascible, I search for my lost innocence. And that is the most difficult task.

Next to a military school are two gardens with exotic plants. A romantic
breeze floats down from them. It's the breeze from my passionate book-filled
youth as well. Sometimes I sit in one of the gardens, and I feel as if my
innocence had disappeared in the same way as the dreams that came to me
from these books.

Sometimes after a long walk beneath the trees, when I arrive at the spot
where the gigantic city spreads out before me, I realize that I have nowhere
to put down my roots. I sit down. In the distance, the lights gradually
turn on one by one, while the buildings sink into the twilight. Here and
there, the windows and the roofs sparkle with the day's last reflections, like
a young woman's naked knees. Having taken over my youth, she is still a
temptress and a curse, a beauty who destroys a man after affording him
untold pleasures. And beneath the red horizon, the city's vampiric beauty
makes us forget home and hearth. She's transformed this oblivion into pure
suffering. Beautiful and evil. Even after she's deceived me, I remain loyal to

her. And yet in spite of this bond, I can't stop my tears from flowing when I hear a song from my native land. I have nowhere to settle down. That's the fate of a man born outside his homeland. I can never abandon her, and yet I know that I must do so in order to create great things. A life of struggle awaits us. The years fly by and make me bitter.

Faced with this city to which I owe every fiber of my being, my soul remains divided. It abounds in pleasures, in beautiful women and poetic autumns. And yet its countless vices fascinate me at times and repulse me at others. The hashish smokers, the beggars, the specialists in eight or nine sexual positions, the homosexuals and the lesbians, the followers of Sappho, the impotents and the syphilitics. I recall the years I spent going from factory to factory, unemployment, the fear of being caught without proper identification papers, situations that were untenable for one's spirit and soul, while the lights grew and slowly multiplied, and the city became a Milky Way. I become excited; filled with both love and hatred, I am incapable of expressing my feelings in words. I look down from the mountaintop; with fear and desire, I observe a soul divided between monsters and God . . .

I look up at the Eiffel Tower, where, in the spider's web hanging from the sky, a light comes on to guide the planes home, as a star once guided the three wise men. Radio waves pulsate, powerful and magical, while I tremble to find *le mot juste*.

I watch, and I understand why my compatriots leave this all behind in order to return home. A dream has collapsed within them. Each one of them recounts his own history of the diaspora and worries about his children. They curse these wonders as they leave them behind. The mystery of their ancestor's homeland draws them away. And each one is proud of his disdain and also excited by the new path he's embarking on. I understand why they fall to their knees once they arrive and kiss the earth. Each one of them carries in his heart a need for justice and for a transcendental notion of humanity. And now he understands that he can find these things in his own country and nowhere else.

On the horizon, I see the procession of pilgrims arriving from all different parts of the great city and its suburbs. Sad and abandoned by them deep within the woods, I observe two clouds play out a frightening scene. One of the clouds stares the other one down like a snake. Suddenly, the other cloud, which resembles a bird, is hypnotized by the snake's gaze and falls into its open mouth. And as the cloud digests its victim, its long tail spread out the length of the crimson sky, like the ancients, I become witness to a cruel oracle and feel sorrow for the pilgrims who disappear in the distance.

And once again, I tremble as I try to find exactly the right words to say to them.

What becomes crystal clear to me at that moment is that an alien and foreign city is infinitely preferable to a homeland where one feels like a stranger and one's freedom is curtailed. On my way back, I recall with sadness a tragic event from my childhood. In order to ensnare some birds, Hadji Panoss would hang a cage next to a branch that he had covered in glue. He would place his most charming canary inside the cage. The bird would play its part, calling out to its brothers and sisters, who would all fall into Hadji Panoss's hands without realizing that the canary that sang such a sweet song was already a prisoner. When I return, I sigh again.

I have nowhere to lay anchor, no safe haven.

18

THERE ARE EVEN LARGER LAKES in the woods that I like to visit from time to time. On one of the lakes, a boat carries two lovers. Around another, they erected an international city, a shining example of human ingenuity, which today has completely disappeared. All that remains is a museum with a zoo. All of the wonders of the world passed by without leaving a trace. All that remains is the zoo. Cars travel down a long avenue, and from above the artificial cliffs, monkeys clap, knock one another around, screech, and pick lice from one another's fur. The bear plunges blissfully into a pool of water. The lion opens and closes his eyes disdainfully, his head resting atop his paws.

All of the wonders of the world passed through here: that colossal and nightmarish structure, the Angkor temple, all of the masterpieces of modern architecture, the souks and rugs of Algeria, the perfumed oils and incenses of the Orient, all of the products made in Africa, Asia, and America. Hundreds of thousands of visitors came to see these things, a paradise with projection lamps and loudspeakers hanging from the trees. Cafés, ballrooms, theaters, boutiques, artistic and industrial treasures. White walls and clean streets. All of the products of civilization and its promises of happiness were here. They disappeared. Material progress wasn't enough. Man also needs spiritual satisfaction and progress. On the lake's barren shore, I mourned this absence deep within me.

One day, it occurred to me that these supposedly wild animals were more authentic than human beings. I heard their cries. The lions' roars exploded against the boulders and rolled through the forest, while the sirens that blared across the capital foretold imminent danger. They passed through the trees like gorgons after calling to one another from neighborhood to neighborhood. The planes' roars approached slowly with the cruelty of a rising sea, like a rotating saw, slicing the sky. As the sirens' truncated heads emitted plaintive sounds like a bull's throat being slit, the birds became increasingly frightened and threw themselves from one branch to another. Women ran for shelter as well, scooping up their children and handiwork. And suddenly, in the empty woods, after a short pause, the first bomb exploded, like the blow from a giant axe. The trees all shook, and one of them fell to the ground, screaming in agony. Red lights rushed about from one end of the city to the other. Some brushed against the treetops as they flew toward the woods. They kept growing in number as the night wore on, blazing through the air. Some fell from the sky slowly, terrifyingly, like planets whose cords had been severed, suddenly descending toward the earth, separating themselves from the celestial firmament. Others much farther down, taken by the wind, glided over the woods, spreading their metallic light. Then, suddenly, the storm burst forth. The bombs falling from above onto the city whirled in the darkness and let forth their fire. From below, cannon fire shot upward like meteors, barely missing their targets. Cannon balls traced the sky, painting luminous lines one after the other, rapid and uninterrupted, like one long, continuous water jet or swarm, from one horizon to the other. One of the lions went berserk from the flames and howled, his mouth open toward the sky, and then threw himself forward and fell into the pit that separated his den from the monkey cages. I saw deer dashing about from fear, fleeing the flashing lights. I saw frightened monkeys flee from the tops of their rocks and a polar bear that kept entering and exiting his cave, nervous and agitated by the strange celestial hive, the pounding of the whirling fireballs and the strange flames that rose like trees to the sky in an instant and then just as quickly collapsed.

The Bois de Vincennes was hell. Two planes pursued each other in the sky. A flame trailed behind one of them and illuminated the trees, which were in turn pierced by an onslaught of artillery shells. Leaves fell to the ground as metal shards hit and broke the branches. My only thought was somehow to get myself underground, as even the moles seemed luckier than I was. Wild beasts were right to fear men, for over the centuries, alas, they'd developed death machines that could one day blow up the entire planet. And yet, in spite of its terrifying nature, the pageant on display was also beautiful. I saw multicolored balls of fire thrown from one side of the sky to the other and the most fantastic forms in the clouds: dancers, roses, bright carousels whirling in the night. My eyes weren't deceiving me. What miracles science could achieve if it used its discoveries for the greater good! As I watched in hiding from a stone culvert, I couldn't help but think that small nations such as ours could no longer hope to be free. The century of the Great Powers was beginning. And the world was headed toward a catastrophic end if these nations didn't find a way to get along. It would have been even better if one of them had proclaimed a universal nation or perhaps a federation that united all nations, so that men's souls could finally be at peace. Small nations would have their proper place as well. I was witnessing the apocalyptic dawning of a new century of scientific and political monsters. This occupied country where I now lived had fallen prey to one of them. And my own small people, who had tried for centuries to lift themselves up only to be beaten back down each time, were anxiety-ridden because from now on, they would have to live at the mercy of stronger nations and renounce all traditional notions of patriotism and independence.

I remained bitter even as Paris was being liberated. Taken by surprise, I found myself caught between combatants fighting from tree to tree. A weak one, with the help of stronger allies, chased the one who had enslaved him, a giant on the verge of collapse. This victory didn't make me happy, because I could already see the shadow of another monster descending on them. Bullets whistled by, propelled themselves forward like vipers, and penetrated earth and tree. Lying on the ground again, I saw tanks emerge from the woods and, more ferociously than the wildest beats, fall and crush the trees that stood in their way. (What a contradiction between this preservation instinct, my desperate thoughts, and my joy.) It was a sunny summer day, and you couldn't help but notice the contrast between the green trees and the red blasting forth from the flame throwers. And after the battle, the blood of fallen corpses spread throughout the woods and on the grass, transforming this contrast into an obvious and moving tragedy.

Therein lie the glory of war and the stupidity behind chivalrous pride. Victory is a sin. And every nation's legends glory in this sin, in blood, and in increasing and repeated misery. When I was a child, I wasn't the least bit patriotic. I also had no idea that there were borders between countries. In school, my history books were the most abstract and incomprehensible. And today I blame them all, now that I understand that these nations were all founded on these types of crimes. They're all guilty of the desire to conquer and subjugate other people, until, little by little, they, too, lose their greatness and collapse from their own wastefulness and debauchery. Guilty, all of the dictators and all of the political and religious truths that fade after having left millions of victims behind to make room for new truths. And my eyes fill with tears as they look out at the meadows reddened with the blood of those who were duped, who were foolish and naïve, as the trees teeter back and forth like the trays on a scale. Every war, every revolution, deceitfully promises to be the last. And the one who sees through the dishonesty of these promises also foresees future wars. Neither faith nor hope can take root inside him. And his sadness and pity turn to anger because of this absurdity which most men openly accept.

And so, on that day, I realized that my people had been the least absurd of all. They had suffered from all of these stupidities and achieved a type of sainthood. They hadn't dreamed of conquest, and they had even felt empathy and sadness in their few victories. Although small and unsung, for centuries, they had been the apostles of the one and only truth, the brotherhood of all men. And seeing that they had suffered because of this mission, that they had been deceived and massacred because of their sincere and naïve impulses, a protest began to grow within me, a passion for justice, a sorrow that progressively transformed itself into the most cruel indignation. I imagined my terrified joy at the destruction of the world. I wanted to watch civilization go bankrupt and self-destruct. At that instant, I wanted to gather up the dead that littered the woods and lead their procession toward the pretentious cities of the past. And at night, after taking long walks, we would sit among the ruins in front of a pyre made from the skulls of vain conquerors, facing a sea of human ashes, and sing the song of vanities and the death of destructive ignorance.

19

IN THE BOIS DE VINCENNES, there is a castle that rises from within it like a submarine. The forest has even spread its greenery to the castle's roof, where shrubs and grass grow side-by-side. Even the tower's stones have turned green with age, sparkling with medieval sadness. The castle pierces through the clouds. From its summit, you can see the entire capital, an immense sea of houses. No longer custodian of the city, the castle stands as a witness to history. What battles it has seen! The stones, covered in the rust that flowed down from the bars on the castle windows, remind one of spilled blood. The walls, worn and dilapidated in places and destined to fall into ruin, make one sad. A final bomb destroyed one of the last walls that still stood there. And the moat that surrounds it, where vegetables grow now instead of water, extends into the castle and leads into the courtyard like a gaping wound. Inside lies a half-burned-down church where princes and knights once knelt in prayer, torches in hand. You can still hear the unsettled hearts of young lovelorn maidens beating with trepidation. And the grass that grows on the roof trembles while the moon's rays shimmer through the bastions where arrows once flew. The fort is a barracks now, where the plaintive song of a soldier's instrument sometimes rises and shines like a dead man's gold teeth. There are many famous prisoners among the dead. They passed through, leaving their names on the stones, including a philosopher whose irony disturbed an entire century. Enemies who once occupied this fort gunned down and buried hundreds of prisoners in its moat. Then, after facing defeat, they, too, were buried near their victims. During this debacle, prisoners were taken from deep within the castle, prisoners whose fear and pallor now made their former pride seem contemptible. Many flags were raised atop the dungeon walls, one more pretentious than the other, and each one was swept away by history. Each victor has the last word, which floats proudly at the tip of a soldier's lance. In the wing that's been transformed into a museum, retreating soldiers left behind a mangled, rusty, and unrecognizable tank. Birds come and go through the barrel of the cannon which once bellowed above the neighboring houses, having crossed Europe and left fiery death and destruction in its wake. In front of it, cars rush by in the street. Life goes on; it flows by.

20

IN SUMMER, the Bois de Vincennes becomes a merciful forest behind my house, surrounding a military hospital. The trees flow through the fevered dreams of soldiers and wounded alike and console them with nature's words, so that they don't wake up to the futility of their sacrifice and feel nostalgia for their amputated limbs. They might see these organs in the hands of some oil baron or black-market profiteer and then cry their sorrow until even the stones are moved to emotion. Every day after midnight, I hear the anguished cry of a bird being dismembered. And this pitiful cry pierces my heart like a knife. Sometimes I rise from my bed and go to my window and approach another tragedy, a collective crime. Yet I see nothing at all. Nothing. Whoever was screaming has quieted down. A velvet silence has returned. The weak don't interest me. The world is tired of listening to our people's lamentations. We are tired of listening to them as well. We wanted to fight, but we didn't know how to organize our battles. We gave the world its greatest heroes, but they turned out to be eagles flying in the hills, brave only in their individual actions. We didn't rise united or avenge ourselves of even a single occupier.

Cowards, betrayed and impotent, we watched as half our people were massacred.

There's a small house in this garden, which for years I mistook for a morgue. Every night, I heard footsteps around it. A door would open, and then I'd hear the sound of a large bag being dragged along the ground. The door hinges creaked. One day, I explained my fears to a friend of mine, a doctor who laughed at me and explained that it was just a storage room where they kept medications. At the hospital, there's an assimilated Armenian woman who is married to a French employee. She has a young child who doesn't speak any Armenian. There's also a wounded Armenian man who has no idea why he went to war in the first place. He knows that he is going to die, and he wants to pass away when that coquettish but friendly Armenian woman who lives on the other side of the building comes to visit. The young man's dream never comes true. The hospital refuses to keep him until he dies . . .

21

I OFTEN WAKE UP in the middle of the night, as if my sleep were cursed. Every dream is a folly, and my dreams are the craziest of all. I awaken to find peacefulness and security in reality. Then I flee reality and try to dive into my dreams to find this peace and security again, but I am unable to. I awaken, my heart beating. A heart that wants to detach itself from my body like a sail from its mast, like a falcon pulling on its leg strap. A heart that tackled me and grabbed me with its ferocious claws. It suffers and in turn makes others suffer; nothing will calm it down. I cannot reason with it. The voice of my conscience passes over all of the ruins that my mistakes, sins, and folly have left behind. It rails against my reason, which slowly chokes it like a tyrant. I fear this tyrant and in my anger want to destroy him. An inheritance from my ancestors that feels foreign and yet is the most authentic part of me. An inheritance sullied by life and by thought.

Torn among these different emotions, during the night's silence, sleep becomes a torture. Sweat rolls down my brow and onto my chest. Alone and abandoned at the end of the world, I'm like a man on death row who doesn't know what crime he's committed. And the wind and the trees' nocturnal whisperings are as merciless as the blade of a guillotine as it's loaded into place. Now all of my inner conflicts clash, and this man born in the dispersion finally experiences the full extent of his tragic fate. Memories shake, persecute, mock, and destroy me. My friends, those who perished, disowned me as they died. Those who survived hide their true feelings. Is it a crime to be self-centered? I despise all of those people who judge me. And yet I would have so enjoyed their trust and empathy! Isn't that where the secret behind my strength and my suffering comes from when I write?

This knowledge fills me with self-hatred. Beyond all of this strength and suffering, where is my true self? I've never had the courage to tell people to their faces what I really think of them. I've never told anyone my innermost desires. And I regret the few naïve, youthful excesses that I committed in the name of art. I suffer from it. Life was a game and a trick. A trick and a game, art. Intelligence was a trick and a game, as well, a collection of foreign elements that undermined our own reality.

Oh, intelligence, my bitter cup! . . .

And yet intelligence is the only thing that might purify one's soul and help one to reach love's consciousness, to heal and calm oneself. I needed intelligence in order to forsake it. Where am I? At the edge of an abyss, in the dark, faced with a temptation that arises from the abyss itself, namely, to abandon my own thoughts and to become a common man. We can't escape the human condition, so why do we insist on trying? Isn't that just vanity on our part, an illusion that springs from our minds, our ultimate pride? So many brilliant minds have come and gone over the years and been completely forgotten. Is suffering worth it? But even this forsaking is a torture. And I know that it's impossible to set foot on the terra firma of deliverance, even when you've seen it from the mountain's peak. Moses broke the tablets. And faced with this impossibility, there isn't a single God to whom I might say, "Father, don't abandon me." There is no wisdom, either, in which I might find refuge. All forms of wisdom are spiritual games and foreign to my nature. A stranger, the wisdom that denies the body and believes only in the spirit and whose abstract words always betray the reality of the flesh. A stranger, the wisdom that wears the Buddha's smile. You can't find true happiness in renunciation or in your conscience. What would men do if they were always happy? Even their reasons for smiling would have disappeared. In order to exist, this smile relies on the stupidities and the misfortune of others, above whom it floats like a light. A stranger, as well, the wisdom that makes speeches about supermen yet makes man act like an animal. That is the lesson of the last war. All those who rule over others are small, bestial, materialistic, condescending, and vain. Intelligence must be the power that conquers vulgar force. I've dreamed of a human intelligence superior even to those of the gods that we've slain, the degenerates whose maliciousness we've witnessed firsthand, superior, as well, to gods that men have created in their own image in order to satisfy their own desires, cruel and good, vengeful and egotistical, at the origin of a dishonest and contradictory religion.

I follow the trail of my own ideas for hours in the darkness, and then suddenly, I awaken. A vein beats against my temple. A danger sign. And suddenly, I am afraid of losing my mind, in spite of all of the suffering it has brought me. What would I be without my intelligence? An even more miserable being, a slave surrounded by jackals, an object of laughter or pity. Something even more insidious than pain, a worm that sneaks between its folds, ice that makes it numb, a spider that transforms the brain into a web. My eyelids contract, burn. Something even more secret than pain. A shard of glass that pierces my brain. And then I am faced with another battle: the struggle for survival. I rub my eyebrows. I squeeze my neck between my fingers. I close my eyes. I stop thinking. But my mind refuses to stay still, even when it's completely lost all reason. It rolls around like a ball of wool, from which rays of light emerge. It's as if I had no control over my own brain, as if it were nothing but a deaf, dark, irritating, repulsive tumor clinging to my body.

And when sleep finally arrives, it's the greatest respite, one that neither love nor glory nor even wealth can equal . . .

22

THE WOODS disturb my sleep.

In the fall, the rain often awakens me during the night. From time to time, water drips down the eaves like blood flowing from a wound. It pours forth like blood from the side of a Jesus still made heavy-hearted by human mystery. In the past, under the falling rain, my little house or the small tent in the vineyard was like Noah's ark in the infinity of my childhood recklessness. I was drunk and happy like a character in *A Thousand and One Nights,* filled with dancing women, narghiles, and fountains. I was drunk and sad in my youth, which I spent in a Parisian hotel: a Baudelairian and Verlainian period. Now, life is a procession of dashing soldiers who will never return home. The rising tide of centuries of misery. Glue that flows down walls and slides down windows. Water that pours into the pierced side of a boat. A wounded bird that falls from the sky and strikes against the courtyard masonry. A surgeon's scalpel inside my flesh, where the cold from the ether spreads its humidity.

When will our slow progress overcome evil and compensate for the loss of our childhood bliss, which it rips away from us as if it were some wretched thing? I'm tired and miserable. When will we salute a human justice come to us from across the oceans? When will I witness a city of reason built upon my forefathers' lands, the only one possible now, one that avoids the pitfalls of independence, when the brotherhood of peoples will rule over us? Homeless and alone, I would like nothing more than to find a homeland that measures up to my dreams. And when will I finally set about the task of building this home, this web of reason, where logic will hold sway? When will I find the proper words to celebrate the fact that my tortured people, after being a victim for centuries of its own self-image, has finally become wise?

I am alone as life mocks, persecutes, and reduces me to nothingness. But still I resist. And this nothingness grows at my expense, developing and increasing steadily with every new generation. It grows brighter and threatens to end with me, and then it surrounds me and threatens to become a torch, spreading fire before it.

It burns and breaks all of the world's taboos by making fun of all of its opinions. It's a time when life and death pass by in waves, and I am tossed from one to the other, slipping from one lie, life, to another, death. And both are powerful. My pride bleeds. The sea reddens before my wide-open eyes. The love of goodness and innocence grows within me. And in this infinite realm that grows and expands, I am but a tiny, forgotten speck. Familiar and unfamiliar faces continue to roll by in waves, faded as in a nightmare; they show joy, derision, envy, contempt, and protest. Transparent as glass, they pass right through me and echo. . . . Now my heart beats like a wound, and my hand searches it out in order to tear it from my chest. The phantom who wants to push me off my chosen path addresses me and attempts to convince me that death is the only possible salvation, the only beauty possible after all of life's ugliness. And just as I feel myself ready to commit this act, I become afraid and look for all of the reasons for death to be just an escape and not a solution. On the contrary, one has to stay behind in order to repair the broken bridges, reestablish the lines of communication and the reign of intelligence.

Now the woman who sleeps by my side has become useless and can no longer save me. Why disturb her well-deserved sleep? And anyway, my suffering makes no sense to her. And thus, as I am holding on by a hair at the edge of the abyss whose moss-covered rock slips through my fingers, time itself seems like another thread ready to break. Its strands come undone, one by one, under my body's weight. I am about to fall. Everything now feels more intense than ever before. Thought follows quickly on the heels of feeling. My entire life becomes undone, spreads itself out, condenses, and becomes a hot spot where the light of truth concentrates itself. And at that moment, my burning soul unleashes its most intense, fiery, bitter burst at beauty. The root of all of my suffering, my failings, and my pains. This thirst of mine for heights has opened before me the deepest and darkest abyss. I've spent my years as a phantom, carrying with me the privation and the pain of an injured people, the waiting, the resisting, the longing for happiness, and I speed toward death without having truly lived. And when I reach the limits of this depression, I begin to see that the most bestial qualities in a man are also the most sensible. I'm jealous of the easy life and of the fact that this man thinks only of himself. I dream of a log cabin deep in the woods, where I might live by myself like a forest keeper, humble and calm, at the lowest rung of humanity. A tiny strip of seashore to sleep by, lulled by its gentle waves, or a hermit's cave where I could atone for the greatest of my sins, the love of beauty. Now my mind (jealously) persecutes its own pride, and my intelligence dies out. It plots against itself, pushing me beyond her, toward my mother and father's God, only to laugh at me a moment later in my defeat. Because at that instant, broken and worn out, I address my creator in order to beg for a bit of peace, for some love and goodness, and to find the faith to be able to love him in return. My thoughts unveil their sharp, diabolical claws and laugh like some hawk-headed Egyptian god. And he speaks the truth. Terrible words: "Now you are addressing someone whom you once thought only the ignorant believed in, and you are doing so only because you are in danger and need something . . ."

And while in autumn this voice rises up with the howling wind, another voice—this one groaning—accepts its misery. These two voices approach and crash into each other. My soul collapses. Even my suffering seems like a sin to me. Prayer is also a sin. Protesting, as well. The creator, if he exists, can only be perfection itself, and a perfect being can neither give nor take. But the voice that begs, so hereditary and natural at that moment, always finds a way to lift itself from all of the obstacles in my thought.

"I've sinned by thinking evil thoughts, by guile, by the desire to harm others, by envy, by jealousy, and by weakness . . ."

And in the distance, one of the trees beats its chest as it admits its past mistakes and faces the darkness lit up by its faith, its eyes crazed, calling out to the other trees again and condemning them to silence.

"By my obscene acts and thoughts toward men, women, animals; toward beasts of burden, night and day, by masturbation and nighttime ejaculation . . . I've sinned with every part and every organ of my body. . . . I've sinned while I walked with my head held high as I dragged myself through the mud, drawn to the right and to the left . . ."

And while the tree tries to disentangle itself with all its might from the earth, my father's image slowly appears. I see him exactly as I did one night, his pale old head bent over a book. He heard me leave my bed but didn't turn around to look at me when I opened the door and entered the room barefoot and made my way toward him. His eyes couldn't see. At that moment, he wasn't the man who had warned his son against the cold, against insomnia and life's dangers, but someone removed from life's problems. He was reading.

Only now do I remember the words to his magic whisperings: "Which one of my sins will I confess to, for my suffering is endless, and my wounds will never heal?"

In his last years, carried away by the image of God, he turned away from men. Did he find his truth, or was this merely escapism? What difference does it make? He followed the path of the sublime. I keep this nostalgic memory of him in my head, but it's all in vain. The message that my father brought me from the depths of night was useless. Useless, as well, the magic words of the prayer that consoled generations past. The whispering continues. And then, at that very moment, a leaf flutters from one end of the courtyard to the other, stops periodically, and engages in a silent conversation with the wind. Constantly arguing, they continue to whirl between the courtyard's four walls. And this one leaf, all by itself, takes on a huge importance. I watch its wayward path through my thoughts, and the idea of sleep and work preoccupies me as well, as do the bitterness that emanates from the workplace and the fear of losing my job. I concentrate only on the leaf, as if it were a fatalistic symbol, the outcome of my entire life's work. Oh! The consciousness that we have of our own misery! But what a godsend my brain is, an imperfect tool that understands its own imperfection and that consoles me by concentrating on a single leaf! A proud tranquility flows through my veins. What great good lies behind this desperation? The miracle slowly unfolds. My taut nerves slowly relax, and the first wave of languorous pleasure courses through my body, a first gentle rocking. My head, which burned from the fiery sands of all of the world's evils, which decreased in size until it was no larger than a shrunken head scalped by an Indian, stops aching. It falls asleep in fits and starts and then awakens again and searches for the sound of the leaf. And the leaf reveals itself, attains the safety expected of it—wisdom, if you'd like—from a little farther on now. And from afar, from my cotton-like lassitude, the last words of this drama can be heard, less effective now.

"You wasted your life. What beauty do you still hope to find? All you can do now is make believe, like the others. (*A silence*). Living means getting down and dirty. . . . And you who have lived to this mature age . . . you can still live some more . . . and that's all that matters."

23

IN THE AUTUMN, I find peace inside an ancient castle.

24

ON WINTER NIGHTS, when the woods are sterile underneath the snow, everything becomes more macabre—vanity's silence. The lakes and the waterfall are frozen over. Even the moon itself smiles with icy teeth. I have no heat at home, so I stay in bed and share the fate of someone buried alive underneath the earth. I suffocate. Daybreak comes late as I wait in my bed. This drama ends when an alarm clock on the floor above me rings. My neighbor gets up to go to work. Things come to life. I awaken momentarily, then fall asleep again in the sweetest of slumbers. I plan to live without hope. That's the beauty of life.

But then, suddenly, I wake up like somebody condemned to staying up late on spring and summer nights. And after fumbling about, I once again recognize the familiar objects in my room. I become accustomed to the time and place that I'm in, and I recognize myself. Then the most terrible battle begins, only to end in the most sublime victory.

25

IN THE SUMMERTIME, the Bois de Vincennes is bewitching.

Enthusiasm always follows on the heels of anxiety.

As dawn approaches, I hear a bird's voice at precisely the moment when, after a night of insomnia, I am headed down the obscure but magical slope toward sleep. I grow larger and larger, like a rolling snowball, gathering up the path's darkness, enveloping myself in visions, simultaneously getting stronger and heavier as I speed down this road toward a precipice. And suddenly, this bird's cry stops me dead in my tracks, as if it were life's crystal reverberating. And then another one spreads out within me like a large neon sign. The darkest corners of my soul and all of my bones light up. It's time for the mystery of mysteries. The air and the trees tremble ecstatically.

The trees speak to one another in surreal voices, recounting unknown stories and occasionally protesting in sweet, if condescending, tones. Sometimes a carefree, crystal-clear song appears out of nowhere, like water cascading forth from a crevice in a rock. Another song appears, this one sad, sweet, and innocent, bright as honey and tranquil like a young girl's song as she awaits to return to her lover. Sometimes the sound of wings proudly and enthusiastically vibrates through the air, followed by a billowing of branches and a burgeoning light, sound and smell crossing thousands of flower buds.

After dark, dawn possesses a graceful beauty. There's a moment of ecstasy between sleep and awakening. Like the sky, it feels as if I am discovering my body for the first time this morning, as it becomes transparent to people and to things. I have the strange feeling of having won a contest. I've uncovered the secret to life's beauty. There are many different dawns. In autumn, they're sublime, soft like the memory of a loved one whose return one anxiously awaits. In the winter, this softness becomes nostalgic in the outside mist, as I dress myself using electric light and go to work before seeing the sun. In the springtime, I already hear my beloved's footsteps. My soul is troubled. And then comes the summer dawn, the most splendid of all. I am engulfed in light. I bathe in the perfume of wild chestnut, linden, and acacia trees. The air around me resounds with the sounds of voices and light that burst forth from tender flutes. It's especially splendid when I don't have to worry about going to work. Far from life, I feel life in its pristine essence, like a grace. It manifests itself in its full majesty when I no longer worry about my often stressful and stupid daily routine, its many joys and privations, about work and earning my daily bread, things that we torment ourselves with our entire lives. Laziness becomes saintly. A victory, a blessing. And from the bottom of my heart, I feel gratitude toward nature and men. After all, would I feel so blessed without them? Laziness is the fruit of our fatigue. Grace is the result of the clash between good and evil. Summer dawn is a great celebration. A righteous and pure calm floats above all of life's falsehoods. A rebirth.

What a moment! I feel as if I were emerging from the depths of a silent ocean. I hear. I feel. The bird songs echo off one another as if they were passing through warm and clear crystal. True glory. An indescribable joy. The emotion of a man who meets his loved one for the first time. A canvas of fear and pain. A canto of drunken love. And all of this grows and spreads out like some luminous vegetation. When confronted with all of these things, inner shadows slowly disperse, abandoning their secret, absurd efforts. They move away like receding waves, like actors leaving the stage, or like evil spirits trying their best to destroy a castle in the dead of night. A bird pursues them, screeching like a wooden whistle.

What a moment! My eyes closed, I glide across infinite and voluptuous space, untying the bonds of my weariness and my troubles one by one, growing lighter and rising toward the light until I am perfectly clear and transparent. And the day's youngest light transforms itself first into the woman of my dreams, then a bird soaring over chasms, then a treetop, and a fountain of kindness. What a moment, when I no longer recognize myself, when I haven't yet assumed my identity and I no longer know where I am. Every single thing becomes absolutely distinct—the beating of a bird's wings as it hops from one branch to another, the leaves shivering, a cat's velvet paws, an iron leash being loosened as it races forward, the noise of a broom reminiscent of a dancer's long dress and of the noise that my mother made as she swept the floor, waking me up every morning for school. Each and every summer dawn, she would sweep the garden clean, and as she approached my window, she would also purify my soul. All of these memories lie within me. The inner and outer worlds are one. There are no borders. I am everywhere at the most distant points on the globe, inhabited by the uncertain memories of the countries and the cities where I've lived, of the countrysides and fields that I've seen, of the trees and roads, of the oceans and rivers that I've known. I'm astonished to be master of all of these things, now that I am removed from them and feel no need for them anymore. Should I conclude that I am closer to the creator now that I no longer think about him and ignore him and no longer pray with self-interest, an egotist who always expects something in return from heaven, or else who rises up against him and, out of misplaced individualism, still resents him for his rejection?

The Bois de Vincennes is bewitching. My experiences have reached a point of almost mystical concentration. I possess the fiery happiness of a believer without actually having any faith. The green from the trees glows differently but remains holy, as well. The city's rumbling takes on another meaning. The light gathering beneath my half-closed eyelids takes on the color of almond blossoms.

This sweetness, a euphoria similar to what a passenger feels when looking out from the prow of a ship after a stormy night as a new city appears on the horizon at daybreak, unknown and promising. The blessing of intelligence that rises again from the ashes. The first emotion of an arrival: alive, vigorous, and victorious. An aurora within an aurora, where body and soul are reconciled and where beauty becomes beauty again and a source of joy. The light that falls on my half-closed eyelids is as white as the marble of the Parthenon. I get out of bed renewed, revived, purified.

And facing the trees, sitting at my desk, my real life begins.

A victory, a grace. Belief and denial are both pointless. I've forgotten all of the lies. Life is new for me, a miracle. I am master of all of my powers. I am overflowing willpower and enthusiasm. A productive force that goes beyond ideals and betrayals, good when confronted with evil, reconciled to the impossible, indifferent to all exterior furor, medium to a sacred mystery, a bee who gives away her honey without thinking, a silkworm that loses itself amid its own threads. A bird drunk on its own crystalline voice.

The Bois de Vincennes transports me to the most extreme ecstasy.

The Bois de Vincennes is bewitching.

The foliage comes alive from the morning heat, expands, fresh, abundant, and sublime, flows over the roofs like a rising tide, and joins the clear and just light, which also continues to expand.

Legend has it that centuries ago, in these woods, under an oak tree, a king named Saint Louis, upon returning from the Crusades and grown wise from defeat, captivity, and liberation, judged guilty men with complete fairness. Sometimes the trees whisper his name when daybreak pierces through them like a ray of light. At that instant, from the depth of centuries, reality becomes legend and legend reality. And in that dreamlike void, life becomes a miracle. That's why every morning, I sit at my desk and become excited again after having criticized enthusiasm and hope, in the name of a pure intelligence devoid of magic. Truth is born of untruth and reverts to falsehood again. But the light that springs forth from truth is beautiful. And so, every morning, my present life progresses in parallel to my childhood. When I wake up terrified, I am the child of days gone by. The next instant, I place before him the memories of my tribulations and defeats, the stories of my capture and liberation. And then the miracle takes place. The child transforms the vitriol from my bitterness into holiness and finds his inner peace. And harmony reigns. The bitterness becomes goodness, compassion, and love for one's country. The woman in my sleep appears more beautiful, more sublime and courageous, more tragic, in fact, because of the pain of childbirth—she is above all men. And my writing, which I know will inevitably fall into the abyss of forgetfulness like all writing, hides this abyss for an instant, as a sacred light does when the aurora penetrates the inner reaches of my soul. And my dreams, on the verge of dying out, are reborn.

The calm after the storm. Blessed be the nascent sun. Blessed be the sacred voice of the white-haired woman who suffers with me, the sincere and good one who utters my name every morning. What would have become of me without her? She is a homeland, a source of hope and energy. She's as pure as the sunlight that comes from on high, and as just. And so, every morning, I approach her with gratitude. Standing before this crystal-like reality, my despair grows into hope and enthusiasm.

The Bois de Vincennes is magical.